Stories by Contemporary Writers from Shanghai

NORMAL PEOPLE

This book is edited and designed by the Editorial Committee of *Cultural China* series

Text by Shen Shanzeng
Translation by Wu Xiaozhen
Cover Image by Kong Derun
Interior Design by Xue Wenqing
Cover Design by Wang Wei

Assistant Editor: Cao Xiaoying
Editors: Wu Yuezhou, Kirstin Mattson
Editorial Director: Zhang Yicong

Senior Consultants: Sun Yong, Wu Ying, Yang Xinci
Managing Director and Publisher: Wang Youbu

ISBN: 978-1-60220-252-8

Address any comments about *Normal People* to:

Better Link Press
99 Park Ave
New York, NY 10016
USA

or

Shanghai Press and Publishing Development Company
F 7 Donghu Road, Shanghai, China (200031)
Email: comments_betterlinkpress@hotmail.com

Printed in China by Shenzhen Donnelley Printing Co., Ltd.

1 3 5 7 9 10 8 6 4 2

NORMAL PEOPLE

By Shen Shanzeng
Translated by Wu Xiaozhen

Better Link Press

Foreword

This collection of books for English readers consists of short stories and novellas published by writers based in Shanghai. Apart from a few who are immigrants to Shanghai, most of them were born in the city, from the latter part of the 1940s to the 1980s. Some of them had their works published in the late 1970s and the early 1980s; some gained recognition only in the 21st century. The older among them were the focus of the "To the Mountains and Villages" campaign in their youth, and as a result, lived and worked in the villages. The difficult paths of their lives had given them unique experiences and perspectives prior to their eventual return to Shanghai. They took up creative writing for different reasons but all share a creative urge and a love for writing. By profession, some of them are college professors, some literary editors, some directors of literary institutions, some freelance writers and some professional writers. From the individual styles of the authors and the art of their writings, readers can easily detect traces of the authors' own experiences in life, their interests, as well as their aesthetic values. Most of the works in this collection are still written in the realistic style that represents, in a painstakingly fashioned fictional world, the changes of the times in urban and rural life. Having grown up in a more open era, the younger writers have been spared the hardships experienced by their predecessors, and therefore seek greater freedom in their writing. Whatever category of writers they belong to, all of them have gained their rightful places in Chinese literary circles over the last forty years. Shanghai writers tend to favor urban narratives more than other genres of writing. Most of the works in this collection can be characterized as urban literature with Shanghai characteristics, but there are also exceptions.

Called the "Paris of the East," Shanghai was already an international metropolis in the 1920s and 30s. Being the center of China's economy, culture and literature at the time, it housed a majority of writers of importance in the history of modern Chinese literature. The list includes Lu Xun, Guo Moruo, Mao Dun and Ba Jin, who had all written and published prolifically in Shanghai. Now, with Shanghai re-emerging as a globalized metropolis, the Shanghai writers who have appeared on the literary scene in the last forty years all face new challenges and literary quests of the times. I am confident that some of the older writers will produce new masterpieces. As for the fledging new generation of writers, we naturally expect them to go far in their long writing careers ahead of them. In due course, we will also introduce those writers who did not make it into this collection.

Wang Jiren
Series Editor

Prologue

Neither "normal" nor "normal people" is an entry in the authoritative Chinese lexicon—*Ci Hai* (*Word Ocean*).

Prologue II

Onlookers don't recognize me. Neither do I recognize myself. Makeup turns me into another person. I become another person.

—A couplet hung on the columns of an ancient stage in Yangzhou city, Jiangsu province.

Prologue III

I used to be sure that it happened in 1964, the year I passed the Secondary School Entrance Examinations—I preferred the phrase "passing the Secondary School Entrance Examinations" to "graduating from primary school" because the former indicated my taking some initiative for the first time in my life. My initiative went nowhere, though. I had aimed at a top secondary school in my district but my scores landed me in an average one. Nevertheless it was all the more memorable precisely because I failed. Human memory is perversely addicted to failure. Biographies of famous people are filled with all kinds of adversities. My biography, if there ever is one, will be the same. Lately I'd been less sure, since it was highly unlikely that I, not yet fourteen years of age in 1964, could have been that mature. Might it have happened two or even five years later? No. After mulling over the events, relevant or irrelevant, that took place afterward, I have decided that it must have happened in 1964, since in following events I seemed to regress from maturity. On the other hand, I don't want to move up my maturity to an even earlier date. Consequently, 1964 became a peak of maturity in my life, an unsurpassable peak no matter how hard I tried later on. However, most probably, I have overvalued the year 1964 in order to commemorate my passing those entrance examinations. Since I need a year to locate the following event, and since no other year is more appropriate, then 1964 it is.

On a summer afternoon in 1964, I took a bath in the back room of my home.

We lived in a *shikumen* (literally "stone gate") house. The traditional *shikumen* houses of Shanghai are as famous as the courtyard houses in Beijing. I dare say I have a better knowledge of such houses than any writer who has written about them. Why are they so famous? Whenever I stepped into the shabby common kitchen whose walls had been darkened by dozens of coal stoves, and whenever I groped my way like a blind person toward the stairwell, which my friends jokingly called a "coal mine shaft," I couldn't help wondering, "Why on earth are *shikumen* houses so famous?" Superior in neither space nor quality, they are artistically mediocre and physically confining to their inhabitants. Moreover, unlike courtyard houses, they don't boast any value in terms of archaeology, folklore, history, sociology, architecture, aesthetics, psychology or ethics. Even so, to the consternation of the elegant garden houses dotting the metropolis, they are known as typical Shanghai houses.

Then one day it dawned on me that they were famous for two reasons. For starters, the First National Congress of the Chinese Communist Party was convened in a *shikumen* house. Secondly, before 1949, only well-off families could afford the rent of one or two gold bars for such housing, while the dog-poor porters, rickshaw pullers, street sweepers and night-soil collectors couldn't. Once categorized as petty bourgeoisie in China, and now called middle class or "white collar" in other countries, these more well-off people make the greatest clamor in society. They view the upper class with both envy and resentment, wanting to join their ranks while clinging to what they already have. Looking the other direction, they regard the lower class with both sympathy and disdain, wanting to help while fearing the risk. They raise a hubbub here and there, and as a result, wittingly or unwittingly, they have conditioned themselves into believing that what they have is the most moderate, reasonable, practical and therefore, ideal. Richer people take delight in encouraging their self-intoxication while the lower class dares not envy their affluence. By and by, their living standards, creature comforts and hobbies have become generally accepted. A case in point: the spiced beans from Shanghai's Town God Temple. Superior to salty fried beans from the Ningbo city (Zhejiang province) but less classy than chocolate sundaes or whipped cream, they used to be the top delicacy in Shanghai. But as times changed, White Rabbit toffees seemed to have become the new rage among well-off families.

The *shikumen* house we lived in was one of the largest. Now twelve families were crammed into the rooms on the first floor and the second floor. The other room on the east side of the first floor had been annexed by the neighborhood factory next door. Except for the original tenant, who had sublet the west wing of the second floor to us, my family had inhabitated this house the longest. Our room, with windows on the southern and eastern sides plus floor-to-ceiling wood panels, was the largest and comfiest of all the rooms. For at least fifteen years my family members were also the poorest inhabitants of this house. While our eleven neighbors packed more children and furniture into their rooms, our bare room, with two apparently ancient folks among its inhabitants, gave the impression that ours was a family that had come down in life.

Our room was partitioned into two by a row of wooden doors inlaid with ground glass panes. The back room, which took up one-fifth of the floor area, was used for storage. A coal stove was placed by its right wall near the entrance. Facing the stove was a gigantic black lacquered square table for eight people. Three cracked boards, each two centimeters thick, made up the table top. The four splayed table legs carried with forbearance their burden: six thermal flasks, an assortment of aluminum pans, several casseroles and earthen bowls, soy sauce, cooking oil, vinegar, cooking wine, salt, sugar, MSG, a mug with some toothbrushes and a tube of toothpaste, two stacks of big bowls and one stack of smaller bowls, a container for chopsticks, porcelain spoons, a rice spoon, a metal spatula, an iron claw, one bottle of mercurochrome and another of gentian violet antiseptic, a tube of sulfathiazole ointment, a bottle of Star Brand toilet water and some rags. On the shelf below the table top were more odds and ends: an iron pan, soap, soap powder, a hammer, an axe, a firewood chopper, a screwdriver, pliers, some used electrical wire, varnished wire, lead fuse wire, adhesive plaster, wood clothes pegs, wooden and plastic combs (some intact, some broken), Pechoin facial cream, clam oil, a small bowl of hair smoother, some old nails and wood screws, corks of various sizes, and so on. On the floor under the table were a carton of coal briquettes, wood chips, waste paper for kindling a fire, tattered clothes that were saved to make mops, a bucket, a wooden tub, etc.

This table helped shape my character. Insignificant as I was, I did share a habit with the Great Teacher of Proletariats around the world. Paul Lafargue wrote in *Reminiscences of Karl Marx*: "Marx had no use for formal symmetry in the arrangement of his books," and "He never allowed anybody to put his books or papers in order—or rather in disorder. The disorder in which they lay was only apparent, everything was really in its intended place so that it was easy for him to lay his hand on the book or notebook he needed." The discovery of these lines in a library as a teenager gave me such ecstasy that I begged my mother to buy me a copy of *Reminiscences of Marx and Engels*. It became one of the first books in my private library. I had received pocket money since fourth grade but my mother kept paying for my books until I graduated from junior high school because, by tradition, I was supposed to save all that money and offer it up to my grandmother at the end of the year in exchange for a word of praise.

The narrow aisle between the stove and the great table was just enough space to fit a wooden tub in which I bathed. Since the wood was semi-finished, before putting it to use every summer we had to soak it in water, for a full day on the balcony, so that the planks would expand enough to stop leaking. My grandmother had developed a habit of showing the tub off to our neighbors on the eve of soaking, because the iron hoop around it had never been replaced since she brought it from Ningbo to Shanghai decades before. There was something special between her and the tub. She died in early 1973. When summer came that year, we put the tub out for soaking as usual. The next morning the iron hoop had fallen apart and the balcony was flooded. Planks lay inside the hoop in the shape of a blooming water lily.

Back on that summer afternoon in 1964, I took a bath in our back room. After arranging the tub between the stove and table legs, I locked both the back door and the partition door. My grandmother asked, when she saw me latching the latter, "Why? Won't it be too hot in there?"

I didn't respond. My heart skipped a few beats. She didn't pursue the topic. My grandpa was taking a nap in the front room. I sat down in the tub. Cool water rose up to my waist. I rubbed myself with a towel. My heart pumped happily. The time was ripe for my experiment.

I had recently found a mysterious source of pleasure down there, but I couldn't tell whether the outcome was urine or not. It didn't feel like urine but I wasn't sure because it usually happened at night. I couldn't rest until I found out.

The experiment went smoothly.

It felt like a lightning strike. Flashes moved rapidly culminating in one place, sparking wild fires along the way. The fresh smell of grass before a thunderstorm permeated the air. A cobweb of blood vessels and capillaries stood out. Hot air lifted my body up. Water whirled joyously in the tub, lapping my smooth back and belly from time to time. A spot of light danced naughtily around my chest, changing colors in a tantalizing manner. My heart melted like ice and then froze over like mercury, reflecting an intense beam of light. My head swam. The fragrance in the air was intoxicating. My eyeballs swelled up like a downy chick about to burst free of the eggshell. I blinked and an invisible fog was lifted forever, a fog whose existence I had been unaware of until then. Now I could see! What an awesome world! Life was more magnificent than any fairy tale, wilder than any imagination! A towering mountain materialized in the turn of a hand. It was overgrown with gorgeous flowers. A multicolored mist enveloped the blossoms. Faintly discernible music rose from behind the mist.

Who cast the spell? Who worked the wonder? Who bestowed divine power on the everyday substances and average cells? Was it me? They were no longer just substances or cells. They were nothing worldly like flesh and blood. They were indescribable! If lightning could be measured, if will power could be colored, then they were lightning and will power. The incredible became credible. The unexpected became expected. The wind was reined. The thunder was hitched to a cart. It was an angel who gave hope of life, but it was also a demon that instilled the fear of death. Overwhelmed by the ultimate mystery and exhausted by all the futile exploration, my thinking self lay down lethargically on the threshold, yawning. My physical self trembled pleasantly and expanded. I saw a little boy whose fat cheeks drooped like those of a turkey. That must be me. He, or I, looked exactly like the snapshot of me taken during my first full month of life. Thumb in mouth, I made a few cautious first steps and then swaggered into a fairyland. All four seasons were present alternately. In the spring breeze, golden butterflies fluttered among bright red corals. Under the summer sun, pythons writhed and turned, exposing silver scales on their bellies and giving off a strong musky smell. In the autumn drizzle, a swan swallowed the last fireball. All its feathers were immediately scorched. It licked the rosy new flesh sighing contentedly. Finally tens of thousands of white rabbits bounced up from underground and turned the earth an infinite white. The white snow felt like hot lava. The magnificent universe and a humble life form became one in that instant. A halo appeared above the volcanic crater.

I sat cross-legged in the tub feeling the caress of water. The potion of life had been added to it. I had been endowed with something new. This new fluid must be more precious than saliva. My grandparents told me never to spit, because saliva was vital to life. Saliva was sticky. This new fluid was much stickier. I suddenly felt hungry. Could I indulge myself this way in the future? All men might have such fluid, but not all men knew such a handy way of getting high. Would it harm my health? Thinking about it, such indulgence in the past had never made me feel worse; instead I had always had high spirits afterward. On the other hand, spitting didn't seem to have hurt my vitality either. How could one tell if one's vitality was intact or not? I would hate to give up my "discovery" for some unknowable risk.

I couldn't ask anyone's advice. This would be the only thing that I could do without permission.

Before I knew it I was singing.

Then I realized I was humming an unknown tune. I might have heard it somewhere or I might be improvising. My singing brought things to life. Grass sprang up in the pond. Birds chirruped in willow trees. A breeze brushed against my wet skin. I felt refreshed. A sweet voice came through the tune to me, "Let it grow. Let it grow." I saw another new thing grow inside my body, like a bamboo shoot breaking through the soil—my talent for music composition! More pleased than ever, I raised my voice. An entire orchestra seemed to accompany me in the background. Then my grandmother dispelled it all.

"Shake a leg. Stop meowing."

I walked into the front room. My grandpa was lying awake on the wooden single bed with four uneven legs. The crisscross coir ropes used to string the bed frame had rotted away, so we had to reinforce the bed with some metal sheets. I sat at the table reading a book with unseeing eyes. After a while, my grandpa got up, put on his cloth shoes with the backs turned in, and walked toward the window. All year round he wore a pair of black cloth loafers. At home he converted them into slippers by turning the backs in. As a result the shoe backs wore out faster than the rest of the shoes. After adding some water to his tea glass, he sat up straight in a chair, collected himself, put one palm on top of the other, and didn't move a muscle. It was his habit to sit like that for hours. According to him, this was how a scholar was supposed to sit: the eyes contemplating the nose, the nose contemplating the mind, the mind undistracted, and the breath sinking to the lower belly. My grandpa had studied in an old-style private school. A lean seventy-four-year-old, he looked like a legendary immortal with his pale ivory skin and white goatee. He walked with a straight back, looking distinguished and aloof from worldly concerns. Strangers would never be able to tell he was just a sidelined patriarch of an impoverished family.

On that afternoon, however, my grandpa opened his eyes wide after sitting for only a while.

"Who was in the back room just now?"

"Me."

"What were you doing?"

"Bathing."

His thoughtful look made me nervous. Did he know? Did my face or body betray me?

He broke the silence. "I had a dream. I was sleeping in the bed. A white glare woke me up. I had no idea where it came from. Then I saw it was from the back room. I got up. The back room was dazzlingly bright. I thought the stove might have caught fire, so I rushed to the door. It was so hot. Sweat rained down my forehead. I pushed the door but it didn't give. I calmed down. Anxiety didn't help. Then I remembered I should pull instead of push. I was right. The door opened. Air gushed out. It was mingled with the fragrance of jasmine. There was a ball of light several stories high in the back room. My eyes were blinded. I wondered how a small back room could fit such a huge ball … Then I really woke up."

He reached for his tea glass, blew on it to help it cool down, and then took a sip. Once the glass was back on the table, he resumed meditation. Catching my mouth agape, I shut it up immediately. Neither my grandmother nor my siblings changed their facial expressions. His words seemed to have gotten lost.

My grandpa never mentioned the dream again.

So two events happened on that afternoon. They might be unrelated but I had a sense that there had been a plan. Of course, strictly speaking, they didn't count as events. No, nothing major at all. Yet something did happen.

The following stories will unfold in a similar pattern.

I

I had no idea what was on other people's minds when they were ordered to work in rural areas. I prayed for World War III.

It was true. Humor was not my strong suit back then.

In April 1970, I hurried home from the state farm where I worked to see my younger brother off to a rural production team. There was little else I could say to cheer him up other than the widely criticized saying of Mencius: "When Heaven is about to confer a great office on any man, it first exercises his mind with suffering, his sinews and bones with toil ..." The initial policy had been for each family to send one child out of every two to the rural areas. Since I was already working on a farm, my brother could have stayed in Shanghai. However, answering the call of Chairman Mao in his "December 21 Supreme Instruction," a group of Red Guards pasted up a "big-character poster," a typical handwritten form of propaganda and communication, vowing to receive revolutionary education in rural China. In their minds, Shanghai, the very cradle of the "January Revolution," was not revolutionary enough. Suburban Shanghai was no good either. They had to leave Shanghai entirely. The Party propaganda department in Shanghai was not offended, but other people, including a male classmate of mine, were. After all, it was only natural for different opinions to exist in a country of 800 million people.

My classmate was barely 1.58 meters, or just over five feet tall in his shoes, so we nicknamed him "Little Muck" after a character in a fairy tale by Wilhelm Hauff. Little Muck was known for his sharp tongue. On the eve of Chinese New Year in 1969, all the students in the graduating class who had not yet been assigned a job were instructed to meet at school to discuss job assignments. They were also told to report to school with a full stomach and in warm clothes. Little Muck sensed something had gone wrong. Yet, shrewd as he was, he couldn't afford to skip it. At 7 p.m., after taking attendance at the school auditorium, the Workers' Propaganda Team stationed at our school locked the doors and took out trays of fist-sized paper-cut red hearts. It was announced that only those students who took a paper heart, wrote his or her name on it, and stuck it to the Allegiance Board could get written permission from the head of the Workers' Propaganda Team to go home.

The auditorium was in an uproar. Hundreds of bodies squirmed like snakes to avoid contact with the paper hearts, thinking that signing one was a sure ticket out to the country to join a production team. The head of the Workers' Propaganda Team shouted Chairman Mao's "Supreme Instructions" into the microphone, from "Revolution is not a dinner party" to "Tell the truth and you'll receive a lighter sentence; resistance can only lead to severe punishment." No student yielded. The team implemented Plan B. They sent the students to their former classrooms. Each classroom was manned by a member of the Workers' Propaganda Team. Little Muck led his classmates to confront Lao Lü, the team member assigned to that room. He complained loudly about the inequity and foul play in job assignments, which Lao Lü countered by saying, "Chairman Mao now calls on young people to work in rural areas. You may disregard other people, you may challenge the Workers' Propaganda Team, but will you defy Chairman Mao?"

Little Muck was speechless. Lao Lü was a stout, swarthy Shandong native. When he first arrived at our school, he had mumbled and blushed as if suffering from congenital heart disease. Little Muck picked a fight with him thinking it was a sure win. To his surprise, Lao Lü was much more eloquent after half a year's time. Other students snickered.

Little Muck blurted out, "To leave Shanghai is to admit Shanghai is reactionary!"

Lao Lü had another heart attack.

Little Muck quoted one Supreme Instruction after another from the "Little Red Book." His arguments grew wilder and wilder. Finally Lao Lü fled the classroom, ashen-faced. Everyone fell silent. After what felt like a century, Lao Lü returned to beckon Little Muck from the door. Having smoothed his parted hairline, Little Muck walked out. The other students saw him off like Communist prisoners in the Nationalist Party prison seeing off the revolutionary martyr, Jiang Zhuyun, on the way to the execution ground. The head of the Workers' Propaganda Team, who was standing behind Lao Lü, smiled at him. Once inside the team's office, he made Little Muck repeat his argument. Then he asked, "What shall we do? If you don't change your mind, we have to report you. Maybe you are right. You are more politically conscious than the rest of us. But what if you're wrong? Do you know what will happen to you?"

Little Muck had no idea. The head told him to chew over it.

When Little Muck returned, defiance had left him. The dozen or so students in the classroom were subdued at the sight of him. Lao Lü had downed two mugs of tea and begrudged talking. By midnight everybody was drowsy. At half past twelve, Robinson was gone. If Robinson had not been a repeater in both primary school and secondary school, he could have graduated in 1965 and avoided all the fuss. Most probably he had scaled the school wall and slipped home.

Lao Lü made another trip to the head of the Workers' Propaganda Team, but he came back with no further instructions from his boss. By 1 a.m., a student who was called Auntie fished out from inside his clothes a baked pancake to eat. He stood out in the class by wearing a dark cloth robe and a pair of saggy trousers, an outfit typical of women fleeing the famine-struck northern Jiangsu province to come to Shanghai, all year round. Usually good natured, he kicked and bit when he was angry. Since his mother was a mental patient, other students usually refrained from provoking him. However, on that night, it was Auntie who provoked others with his pancake. Many complained loudly about hunger.

Lao Lü didn't budge. "You were told to come with a full stomach. What's more, it's up to you whether to go home or not."

By a quarter to two, some students were too hungry to resist. After signing a red paper heart as perfunctorily as possible, they went home. Little Muck asked his buddy Honey Melon to bring a message to his parents to let them know he was alright. He also asked for food and clothes.

Honey Melon went to Little Muck's home at 2 a.m. The latter's mother had been sound asleep, and became anxious when woken. She calmed down upon learning that nothing serious had happed to her son, except that he couldn't leave school. She asked Honey Melon to deliver a full kilogram of parched flour snack and a cotton jacket issued by her husband's work unit. When Honey Melon made his way back to school, it was already 3 a.m., and too late. Little Muck, and the other students who refused to sign, had eaten pillow bread provided by the Workers' Propaganda Team on credit. It cost them 1.2 jiao (1 jiao equals to 0.016 US dollar) and one hundred grams' worth of grain coupons. But they were allowed to eat without paying the money and the grain coupons. Auntie got his share, which greatly impressed the other students who had thought he was batty.

Honey Melon delivered the parched flour and the jacket, but he forgot to obtain new written permission to leave school. As a result he was stopped at the school entrance and didn't leave school until 4 a.m., after much explanation. By 5 a.m. the Workers' Propaganda Team summoned all the diehard students to the auditorium, telling them that signing the heart was only a way to pledge allegiance to Chairman Mao and the policy of sending urban youth to work in rural areas, not an official enrollment by any rural production team.

Little Muck cried out, "F--k! Why didn't you tell us earlier? Everybody would be home now."

The policy of sending urban youth to work in rural areas affected some students in the class of 1967 and the majority of the class of 1968. For the class of 1969, there was no escaping. This was going to be a long-term policy, as long as it took to realize the rule of Communism. No one could stay in Shanghai unless he or she was physically disabled. Anyone else who stayed cheated the pioneers. Those already working in rural areas received the news with mixed feelings.

As soon as the policy came out, my younger brother applied to work on a rural production team in northern Anhui province. In a month's time, he was ready to depart, one of the first in his school. Like me, he had acted promptly. Only losers were supported by their parents, and our mother could hardly support an idle son, anyway. When school was out between 1967 and 1968, I studied Chinese chess. The key lesson I learned from the manuals was that if your opponent announced a check, and if your general could only move in one direction, you must move it without hesitation. However critical the scenario was, you must save the general first. Otherwise the game would be over.

When I got home, my brother's name had been removed from our household registration booklet, his bulky luggage had been delivered to a depot, and his train ticket had been put into his newly bought plastic wallet. In the wallet there was also a crisp ten yuan bill (1 yuan equals to 0.16 US dollar) and ten kilograms' worth of grain coupons, for emergencies. It was time to consider the next move.

I took my brother to the People's Square, where you could look up at the biggest stretch of unobstructed sky in Shanghai. Having worked on a farm for over a year, I felt stifled whenever I came back to Shanghai on holiday. Back in our room, I had to throw both south windows open. Even so, it still felt stuffy. I called it Pulmonary Fresh Air Syndrome. I didn't recover from it until I was transferred back to Shanghai permanently.

Valiant sentiments were only proper under that big stretch of sky. "Why should you linger at the fork of the road, wiping your tears like a heart-broken child?" This poem was about bidding farewell to a friend, which was just right for the era. I had quoted it on dozens of occasions. No wonder it appeared second in *One Hundred Selected Tang Poems* published by Zhonghua Book Company in 1959. I have to compliment the editor-in-charge's insight here. This thin collection of poems starts with *A Political Prisoner Listening to a Cicada* by Luo Binwang: "Who knows if he be singing still? Who listens any more to me?" A very appropriate poem for those people labeled, out of blue, as Monsters, Demons or Capitalist-roaders at the beginning of the Cultural Revolution, who sincerely repented. The second poem in the booklet is Wang Bo's *Farewell to Vice Prefect Du Setting out for His Official Post in Shu*: "Red Guards, don't lose your optimism on your exile." Chen Zi'ang's *On a Gate-Tower at Youzhou* comes third: "Where, before me, are the ages that have gone? And where, behind me, are the coming generations? I think of heaven and earth, without limit, without end. And I am all alone and my tears fall down." People felt all the more lonely in the midst of sound and fury. Was there anything wrong? The fourth poem was He Zhizhang's *Coming Home*: "I left home young; I return old." People dismissed from office returned, and people sent to work in rural areas returned, but their green years would never return. Coming next is Meng Haoran's *Stopping at a Friend's Farm House*: "We watch the green trees that circle your village, and the pale blue of outlying mountains." People longed for a peaceful, well-off life. The sixth poem is Meng Haoran's *A Spring Morning*: "I awake light-hearted this morning of spring, everywhere round me the singing of birds. But now I remember the night, the storm, and I wonder how many blossoms were broken." People came to detach themselves from history. These six poems tell so much about the vicissitudes of life. It is claimed nowadays that there were foretellings of the Cultural Revolution in Buddhist scriptures and *Tui Bei Tu*, a Tang dynasty prophecy book. I wonder if this poetry booklet was also a prophecy book.

Well, back then I liked to quote Wang Bo because I didn't know how to handle tears. I was terrified of the tears of people parting ways forever, because I couldn't empathize at all. I cried at the wrong time and in the wrong place. On occasions where I was supposed to cry, emotion as well as tears failed me. I was so embarrassed that I wished for a mask.

However I was ready to cry that night. After all, there was a special bond between my brother and me. When we were little, our grandparents forbade us to hang out with the rough kids in the neighborhood. So we were stuck with each other. We used to play table tennis for hours with sheet-iron paddles on the one-meter-round dinner table. We invented our own rules to distinguish our "Cosmos Ping Pong" from "Earth Ping Pong." We grew apart after I entered secondary school, because I had to attend school all day long and do my homework until 9 or 10 p.m. Yet he tagged along when I went to the houses of my close friends from school. In the early days of the Cultural Revolution, I was expelled from school. He joined me on trips to exchange revolutionary ideas. During that time, Red Guards on such trips could use public transportation for free, and they had access to all work units they wanted to visit. The two of us visited Fudan University, Jiaotong University, Tongji University, East China Normal University, Shanghai Normal College, Shanghai College of Foreign Languages, Tianma Film Studio, Haiyan Film Studio, Shanghai Film Dubbing Studio, Shanghai Animation Film Studio, the Writers' Association and Artists' Association, Shanghai Shaoxing Opera Troupe, Shanghai Opera Troupe, Aihua Shanghai Opera Troupe, Qinyi Shanghai Opera Troupe, Shanghai Pingtan Balladry Troupe, Shanghai Farce Troupe, Dagong Farce Troupe, Dazhong Farce Troupe, Shanghai Symphony Orchestra, Shanghai Conservatory of Music, Shanghai

Acrobatic Troupe, and Shanghai Magic Troupe. We saw many famous Monsters and Demons and got a lot of good gossip, such as: The highest pay for a movie script was 50,000 yuan; there was an actor with three wives; and "scratching in the ashes" stood for adultery between a father-in-law and his daughter-in-law. What eye opening experiences they were!

Still later, I went to Shanghai Electric Machinery Plant for further exchange of revolutionary ideas, not to gain industrial production experience as part of secondary school curriculum. My brother was with me too. We brought our own bedding and self-financed the entire stay. The plant was located in Minhang, considered a rural area of Shanghai at that time. More than a month later we set off for home happily, because we had finally stepped out of downtown Shanghai.

My grandparents had always insisted that he addressed me as "Elder Brother" rather than just "Brother," although I was the only other son in the family. I didn't realize the significance of that title until I became an adult: An elder brother assumes the responsibilities of a father to younger siblings. Therefore, on that night at the People's Square, I had to act not only as a loving brother but also a loving father. Wearing these two hats might finally induce some tears from my unfeeling eyes. Indeed, when I sniffed, my eyes tingled. I was relieved. If my brother was going to cry, I would sniff and quote a line by the so-called Sharpshooter Old Lady to the martyr Jiang Zhuyun: "Now, now. Have a good cry because we're family."

However things didn't work out as expected. My brother didn't want to cry at all. He dominated our conversation and there was only one subject: himself. He had learned to inscribe Chinese characters in imitation Song dynasty style neatly onto a wax paper for printing. He had tried inserting acupuncture needles into acupuncture points in people's abdomens. When I reminded him that he had to get used to eating yams on the farm, he said he planned to sell dried yam strips in the city in exchange for rice. Not wanting to dampen his enthusiasm,

I tried to draw his attention to some lessons I had learned the hard way. These were: Don't ever discuss anything controversial behind closed doors on a farm; go out onto a dam or in the fields. Moreover don't ever discuss anything important with more than one person at a time. With three people or more, there is always the risk of a whistleblower. If there are only two people, denial is easier. You could even make a false countercharge.

I poured my heart out to him, feeling as sad as the Tang dynasty poet Wang Wei when he bade farewell to his friend: "Out west where you go, what friendship is there?" A more sensitive listener would have reacted by crying out loud, and then I might have shed a few tears as well. No, not my brother. After acknowledging my kindness by a perfunctory nod of head, he directed our conversation back to himself: He had bought a second-hand multimeter from the Central Market that morning, which he planned to convert into a transistor radio during his free time on the farm.

How annoying! As an elder brother and a longtime pal, and now with firsthand knowledge of farm life, I deserved a more attentive audience. I must drop a bomb on this smart ass. So I said, "We're not going to spend our entire life in a village. It's impossible ..." I knew it was a cliché, but somehow I hoped that repetition would bring inspiration, the way you keep striking a flint to get fire. It worked! Unlike my brother, my brain didn't let me down. After repeating the statement twice, an idea struck me. I got it out as quickly as you catch fire with tinder. "We're not going to spend our entire life in a village, because a war will break out, the Third World War." My brother's eyes lit up at once. Now I had his ears.

"Why do you think the government builds bomb shelters and relocates factories from the coastal areas to the back country? Is it really a waste of money? I hear that the biggest bomb shelter in Shanghai is located right under our feet at the People's Square. Four Jiefang Brand trucks can run side by side in the tunnel. Any why was the Ninth National Party Congress top secret? We heard about it only after it was over. Thousands of delegates sneaked into the Great Hall of the People. This was unprecedented. Why? Just in case the Soviets dropped an atomic bomb.

"China has the best spies in the world. Secret agents employed by the Soviet Union and the US are no match at all. Earlier in the Cultural Revolution, family members of counterrevolutionaries were publicly denounced, but some so-called counterrevolutionaries actually worked undercover for us in Taiwan. When the Public Security Bureau stepped in to protect those family members, the Taiwan government was alerted. Our spies were immediately executed. They had all been senior army officers in key positions. You see, Taiwan spies are still active on the Mainland despite the thoroughness of the Cultural Revolution. Our spies are undeterred over there, too. They have been lying low for decades and could stay so for decades to come. Chairman Mao wants us to be prepared for war and natural disasters. Now you know why."

My brother was now impressed. Basking in his adoration, I did a critical analysis of recent world history—the Middle East, Vietnam, the Berlin Wall, the Cuban Missile Crisis, Chairman Mao's prediction of another world war ("When swallows fly close to the ground, a rainstorm is in the making"), Yamamoto Isoroku's surprise attack on Pearl Harbor, and Mikhail Kutuzov's setting Moscow on fire. My brother drank in my words. He was convinced that the Third World War would break out in one or two years at the earliest, seven to eight years, the latest. By that time, everybody would be drafted into the armed forces. Poor eyesight and bad class status would become irrelevant, because all men are equal in the face of a war. What a fascinating time it would be!

"This war is going to be the bloodiest ever. According to Chairman Mao, two thirds of the world population will be eliminated." Awed by my own words, I knitted my brows solemnly.

"Once the war breaks out, communication may be cut off immediately. So here is what we should do—if either of us survives the war, we should run a Search Notice in a local newspaper everyday for a week. When peace returns, we should go to a library to check all the back issues of newspapers published around the country. If there is such a notice, we will know how to contact each other. If there isn't, then one of us is dead. What do you say?"

"What if there is no local newspaper?"

"Impossible! But it may take some time for the newspaper to resume operation ... Okay, let's do this. We wait until a month after the war is over, and then we run the Search Notice for a week."

"Why not a month?"

"That costs too much. They charge a lot for a notice. What's more, the war just ended. One week is enough. Even if we don't read about each other's notice in time, we can always look it up later. The odds of reading one notice out of seven should be pretty high."

"Then why not run the notice on alternate days? We could stretch seven days into half a month."

"No! Don't complicate things. If we run the notice on alternate days, we have to keep reminding ourselves every other day, and we may forget. So a month after the war ends, we run a Search Notice for each other every day for a week. Got it?"

"Got it."

There was a faint smile on his face. I decided it was a smile of anticipation, not a jeer or a forced smile. He looked into my eyes, indicating he was indeed serious.

II

One week before job assignments on graduation in early fall of 1968, Mr. Jin, one of our two class teachers, was suddenly hospitalized for acute hepatitis. While a virus targeted his liver, Destiny's first volley of guns targeted me.

So far in my life, I had been surrounded by Destiny believers without giving up my rational, materialistic position. But this time I was bombarded from my bearings.

Both my grandparents were devout followers of the Goddess of Mercy, which I had previously, wrongly, equated to the worship of Buddha. They recited the *Prajna Paramita* (the famous *Heart Sutra*), one of the scriptures obtained by Tang Monk on his historical pilgrimage to India, at least once a day. They worshipped the Goddess because she was infinitely merciful, helping people in distress, turning calamities into blessings, and rewarding her disciples with benediction and longevity. Recently I studied the *Diamond Sutra*. "This is so I heard," Buddha said, "if a Bodhisattva believes in the notion of an ego, a personality, or a living being, he is not a true Bodhisattva." He also said, "He who sees me by outward appearance, or seeks to hear me speak, loses the path, and cannot realize the fully enlightened one." In other words, it is against the Supreme Enlightened Mind to pray for blessing, longevity, avoidance of disasters, offspring, wealth, a bright future, or smooth going. Buddha will not bless you with mundane happiness, fulfill your worldly desires, or give you a better afterlife. Buddha only wants you to grow disillusioned with the mortal world and then accept his guidance into the void. Nirvana is possible for all living beings, but it is not granted. If you follow this logic, then the more my grandparents worshipped Buddha, the more sutras they chanted, the further away they were from Buddha. Isn't that strange? I guess there must be some different rules governing the worship of the Goddess of Mercy. Otherwise my grandparents would have been greatly wronged.

They had unparalleled faith in the Goddess of Mercy. In the height of the attack on the "Four Olds"—old ideas, old culture, our habits, old customs—they simply rolled up a hanging scroll of the Goddess and put it away, and moved a porcelain statue of her to the top of a black lacquered glass case in the center of the room. Before that, both objects were placed in the northwestern corner of our front room. The hanging scroll draped down the wall, and the porcelain statue was on an eye-level shelf, protected by a glass case. When we kids were little, the shelf obstructed our view. All we saw was a square of ceiling darkened by candles and incenses, which made the corner even more awesome.

Nobody cared to touch anything even years after my grandparents had passed away. I didn't lay my eyes on them until we had to remodel the room for my wedding. The hanging scroll turned out to be a shoddy woodcut on some cheap rice paper, and the porcelain statue was much inferior even to those sold by street vendors. Although I realized that the make of the idol was not that important to the faithful, I found it embarrassing that my grandparents had paid homage to such poor representations of the Goddess all their lives. I had even entertained the idea of buying a fine painted porcelain statute of the Goddess to put on our chest of drawers in memory of my grandparents. But of course I didn't act. The shelf, which had later served as home to their cremation urns, was removed as part of the changes for my wedding.

Back then, my grandpa got up at around 5 a.m. and went immediately to offer incense to the Goddess of Mercy, without washing his face or using the toilet so that he, like *qigong* practitioners, could worship with the vigor accumulated throughout the night. He worshipped standing. First he kindled three "Indian Agalloch Eaglewood Incense" sticks (later renamed "People's Sanitary Incense"), waved them across the air in an arc to snuff out the fire, and let the white smoke rise. Then, with incense sticks between two palms, he bowed his head and prayed silently. Sometimes if I woke up early, I would spot his dark profile against the early morning light coming through the southern window. He looked like an old tree. What impressed me the most was how he looked in his checkered silk Chinese-style summer frock. His bony figure, billowy frock, and the faint fragrance of incense felt so reassuring that I almost always fell asleep again.

Since my grandmother worshipped later, at around 8 a.m. after a trip to the wet market and a thorough cleaning of the room, her rituals left a deeper imprint on us. She worshipped kneeling, chanting and kowtowing at the same time. She had her own ritual supplies: a thin yellow damask cushion, a string of wooden beads (sandalwood, according to her) whose ginger paint was chipped, and a sheet of scripture with images as well as text. She would kneel on the cushion, the beads in her hand and the scripture spread out in front of her. When I grew up, I always wondered about the scripture. My grandmother was illiterate. Even so, wouldn't she have been able to memorize the text after years of chanting? It's a pity I never found out why.

It was not that I couldn't find out but that I didn't want to know. Back then, I froze when my grandparents mentioned the Goddess of Mercy, or the White Lady, to me. In my mind there were three missions in life: getting myself recruited by the Young Pioneers, the Youth League, and then the Communist Party. I was afraid of finding myself in the same predicament as my mother. My mother became a Youth League member shortly after the Liberation. In 1955 she had to withdraw from it because she was overage. Afterward she submitted applications to the Party repeatedly. However at the same time she followed her parents' practice of abstaining from meat on certain days, the details of which, despite my grandpa's instructions, were lost on me. Only three dates stood out in my memory—the nineteenth day of the second, sixth and ninth month of the lunar calendar year. These were all supposed to be the birthdays of the Goddess of Mercy. I asked my grandpa why she had three birthdays, to which he responded, "Because she is Bodhisattva." I also understood that there was one extra date particular to our family—the birthday of my grandpa's mother, who had been the first in the family to use the date-specific vegetarian diet as a way to show filial piety to her mother. My grandpa adopted the practice to show his devotion to his mother, and then my mother had to follow suit in order to be filial to him and to my grandmother.

Later, when I read *The General History of China* by Fan Wenlan, I jumped at the lines stating that Buddhism was actually against filial piety, because it regarded the mortal life as a prison and urged people to become monks or nuns in order to disentangle themselves from worldly shackles. Despite my grandparents' wish I discontinued the family tradition. My mother said, "I'm practicing it now, my children don't have to. They are going to take up jobs and eat in canteens. They won't continue, because canteens cook vegetables in lard. Starting a practice and then breaking it is worse than never starting it." My grandmother agreed. Since she agreed, my grandpa agreed, too.

Nevertheless my grandpa never stopped trying to convert me. He did this by telling me stories. There were two types of stories he used. The first type was taken from *Ghost Stories* and a series of five legend collections from the Ming dynasty, all sporting the theme of karma or enlightenment after meeting an immortal. I listened for fun because as a third or fourth grader, I found books printed in traditional Chinese characters in a vertical form challenging. My grandpa didn't point out the morals in these stories directly, though. Later, when I read those books myself, I found some familiarly strange stories. I might have heard them from Grandpa but his versions were not identical to the books.

Even so, his stories did have an effect on me, although for a while I had considered his attempts futile.

The second type of stories was derived from his own life. There were only two in my memory, because they were too distinctive to be forgotten. However there was something illogical here. If he wanted to captivate me with such fascinating stories, he should have told me more. Why were there only two? Was the rest of his life just boring? No, I remembered clearly on that day he said he was going to tell many more similar stories later. Yet he seemed to have gone back on that statement. Or probably it was me. My indifference might have hurt his self esteem.

I remember I was ill that day, moaning and groaning in bed with either a fever or some physical pain, maybe a toothache or stomachache. My grandpa came over.

"Why don't you chant some sutras? It helps."

I put on a look of scorn. He laughed and said, "Well, you don't believe me, do you? I know. This stuff works only for believers." It may seem surprising that he said "stuff" since the term is often derogatory in Mandarin. But it is a neutral term in my grandpa's Ningbo dialect, so it was not blasphemous for him to refer to the practice of Buddhism as "stuff."

"I've been a believer since I was little. Now let me tell you two stories. You'll see how the Goddess of Mercy saved my life."

He sat down confidently by my bed, similar to the way he gloated over a chess game I was soon to lose.

Story Number One took place during the War of Resistance against Japan, when he was a self-employed trader traveling between Ningbo and Shanghai. According to my grandpa, the life of a traveling trader was almost as dangerous as that of guerillas. I asked why he hadn't joined the guerillas anyway. He said Chief Huang of the Communist Siming Battalion used to be a shop assistant at the joss paper store next to the box business owned by his father. The two of them had been friends since childhood. Chief Huang had always been the shoddiest kid among their gang, with a runny nose all year round.

So he bypassed my question, and I didn't pursue it. There was no point goading him into some improper remarks that might be overheard by neighbors.

My grandpa dealt in silver and gold, the riskiest of all trades. Anyone caught by the authorities would be executed by being shot on sight. On that day, when the bus he took arrived in Shanghai, the entire parking lot was surrounded by Japanese military police carrying loaded guns. All passengers were to be frisked. It was too late to get rid of the twenty-four silver bars tied to his torso. The bus pulled over. Passengers got off one by one. He lingered at the end of the queue, but in a minute the Japanese would search him. He appealed to the Goddess of Mercy in desperation by reciting silently the *Heart Sutra*. No sooner had he stepped down than an uproar broke out at the entrance: men shouting and dogs barking, followed by a gunshot. The gunshot sounded like a slap on his belly, and he immediately felt the impact. His bladder distended and he wanted to pee. The Goddess must have heard his plea!

Losing no time, Grandpa walked toward the back of the bus and crossed to the other side. The conductor cast him a look but soon lost interest when Grandpa made to unbuckle his belt. No one else, including the passengers ahead of him and the Japanese military policemen, saw him. Close to the other side of the bus was the wall of the parking lot, and in the wall there was a hole large enough for him to scramble through. He had barely straightened himself when a rickshaw for hire approached. He hailed it, haggled over the fare for a bit, and then got on. After a while it grew dark but the surroundings were more and more deserted. This was not good. Maybe the rickshaw man, having seen him flee through the hole in the wall, planned to murder him for his money in some place quiet. Again Grandpa started to recite silently the *Heart Sutra*. As he did so he removed a silver bar without the rickshaw man noticing. Roughly twenty-five centimeters in length, the silver bar had the thickness of a bamboo pole (the type used to air-dry laundry) and two pointed ends. There was also a little hook on one end. He hid it in his right sleeve just in case. The rickshaw got to a railroad crossing. Grandpa stamped repeatedly for the man to stop. The man wondered aloud why, because they hadn't arrived yet. Grandpa paid and left anyway. He didn't relax until he made sure nobody was chasing him. Later, when he asked directions, he found that the rickshaw man had indeed made a detour, and that a new checkpoint had been set up on the old route.

The second story was even more incredible. In the first story he took a bus, while in this story he took a boat. In the first story he was alone, while in this story he was traveling with his wife and daughter. In the first story he tied goods to his torso, while in this story he packed goods in several suitcases. If he abandoned the goods, the entire family would be reduced to ruin and poverty. If he kept them, the Japanese soldiers and Chinese army collaborators stationed at the port would kill them all.

As the port drew closer and closer, my grandmother and mother huddled in fear. Remembering what happened the previous time, my grandpa started to recite silently the *Heart Sutra* again. The boat pulled in to shore. The passengers in their cabin had trickled off, but the three of them were still huddled together chanting the *Heart Sutra*. Then the Goddess of Mercy appeared in the disguise of a policeman in a black uniform.

"What's wrong? Why are you still here?"

"She feels dizzy." My grandpa pointed at my grandmother. "We'll wait it out."

My grandmother was so pale that she looked indeed like someone in shock.

"Where are you going?"

My grandpa suddenly saw a light. "To Zhou's Jewelry Store."

"Who do you know there?"

"Scatterbrain Zhou," my grandmother answered.

"Mr. Zhou, the boss," my grandpa explained. My grandmother had been so dazed that she had blurted out Mr. Zhou's nickname.

"Who is Mr. Zhou to you?"

"He's a relative."

The policeman nodded, "Are all these suitcases yours? Put them together and stay where you are. If someone else challenges you, tell him Constable Guo ordered you to wait here. I'll be back in a minute."

After a while another policeman came over to demand their departure. My grandpa answered as instructed, to which the second policeman responded, "Bullshit. Follow me!" They had no alternative but to follow him, luggage in hand, down to the bottom part of the ship. To their surprise, Constable Guo was there.

Boats traveling regularly between Ningbo and Shanghai had huge portholes in this part of the ship. Constable Guo propped open one of them, whistled, and a dinghy shot across the river at once. Constable Guo told Grandpa to pass all the luggage onto the dinghy before bringing his family over. As Grandpa planted his feet on the dinghy, a steamer trudged toward them. His legs jiggled so much that he almost fell overboard with my mother in his arms. The dinghy pulled away from the boat and dropped the three of them off at shore, unguarded. When they arrived at Zhou's Jewelry Store, Scatterbrain Zhou said he didn't know a Constable Guo.

"What?"

"Whooooa, did you see it coming? Your grandpa is old now, but there are still many things I can't explain. Young as you are, how dare you challenge the unknown? Other people may lie to you, but would your grandpa lie to you?"

I was dumbfounded. I mean, I was not converted yet. Just look at the two disciples of the Goddess of Mercy right in front of me, who had nothing to be proud of except their gray hair. However, unease was growing inside me like a mist. It would linger for many years to come.

Grandpa wasn't done yet. "Do you feel better? It's better, right?"

Discomfort returned at once, but moaning and groaning so soon would embarrass Grandpa. Grandma intervened in time, "Why do you bother him with old stuff? He is just a kid. What if he tells other people? Religions are out now. Grandma knows better than your grandpa. The Goddess no longer makes appearances. Instead stars come down to earth ..."

"Stop right there. Do you really know better than I do? That big mouth of yours. Stars coming down to earth? I told stories just to distract him."

They started to argue with each other as to which topics were taboo. I turned to face the wall. Someone on the other side sneezed into his or her handkerchief. I moaned in a loud voice.

My grandparents used to be politically savvy, but as they grew old, they were increasingly careless. Grandma was wise enough to hide the statue of the Goddess of Mercy during the movement against the "Four Olds," and shut the door during her rituals, but then at the same time she drew attention to her callused knees because they were proof of her faith. Grandpa was no better. On one hand, he warned me against offending the Red Guards because they would search our house, confiscate our property, hang an incriminating sign on our door, and shave half of our hair. On the other hand, he told the old lady who sublet the room to us that the wife of Chairman Mao used to be a starlet in Shanghai with the stage name of Lan Ping. He even hummed a tune Lan Ping had once sung. The troubles they gave me!

III

A major reason why I told my grandparents about Mr. Jin's hospitalization was because I was late for supper one night and looked upset. I wanted them to believe that I had spent the afternoon discussing such a serious issue with my classmates. They were convinced, partly because I had never been known to tell lies.

"Don't worry and don't panic," Grandpa said. "It's no big deal. I told you this before. Don't ask for trouble and don't shrink away when trouble comes. Now eat. I'll figure out something afterward."

Then with a smile he watched me eat. I had to remember table manners despite my hunger. It took me ten minutes to finish two bowls of rice. Without him watching I would have gobbled them down in five.

After supper he had me drink from his tea glass, because sorrow was bad for the digestion. I had always drunk from his glass behind my grandmother's back. If she saw me do it, she would scold me for being unhygienic. Nevertheless I had picked up the habit when I was six. Water was too bland to my taste, but I was not old enough to have a cup of tea every day.

He made me sit across from him and regarded me with a smile. His gray-haired head seemed to move in an imperceptible swing at a high frequency, the way a burning briquette gives off faintly discernible heat. I felt the legs of my stool bend and twist in the heat.

"Do you know where Ms. Dong lives?"

I thought there was a slip of tongue. He had named another teacher, but he must have meant Mr. Jin. "Yes. I've been there. On East Jinling Road."

"Good," Grandpa said. "You need some gift. Let me think. Some fabric will be fine. I wonder if they still carry Melton. Buy enough for a lady's short overcoat. At most it costs fifty yuan. I'll pay. I've been saving almost ten jiao out of my monthly pension. Also we could sell my overcoat to a thrift shop. A length of fabric. That's it!"

It was not until then that I realized he had indeed meant Ms. Dong. Gasping, I sucked back my snot so hard that tears almost welled up.

"Look at you," Grandpa's long-nailed right index finger and middle finger almost touched my forehead. "Out of your wits again! What are you afraid of? I don't get it. Where's your usual mature self? I'm asking you to send a gift, not to break into her house. What's the big deal?"

Was he suggesting bribery? Bribery was no better than burglary!

"I don't know where she lives."

"Didn't you just say yes?"

"I thought you asked about Mr. Jin."

"Mr. Jin. Well, Mr. Jin. Pay a visit. Bring him some glucose or milk powder. That's enough. Mr. Jin and Ms. Dong don't see eye to eye, do they?"

"That's what my classmates say. I don't see it that way myself."

"Listen! When will you get smarter? Being dumb is one thing but being deaf to advice is another. A smart ass has a rough life. You'd better listen to me and pay Ms. Dong a visit. It will pay off."

I shook my head firmly. Grandpa was on the verge of a stomping fit.

"You silly kid!" His long fingernails brushed against my lashes and nose.

Grandma came to my rescue. "You can lead a horse to water but you can't make it drink. He's not made that way."

"This should be a piece of cake. Is it hard to do? Not at all!" Grandpa pursed his lips as if to suppress a cough. "If you're cowed by such a simple matter, how are you going to confront life!"

"Gifts are out nowadays." Illiterate though she was, Grandma sounded more insightful than Grandpa, who read newspapers every day.

"Out? From ancient times to the present day, ass kissing has never been out! Even Yama, the lord of death, likes it. Beggars can't be choosers. The Qing dynasty, the Taiping Heavenly Kingdom, the Japanese Invasion, I've seen it all. How does the present differ from the past? Even that Ming dynasty paragon of honesty, Hai Rui, is under fire now ... All right, all right, I'm off topic. You, find out where Ms. Dong lives and accompany me there. If you dare not go alone, I'll go!"

I shrugged. It didn't matter which of us went.

"What? You don't like the idea? Tell me what's on your mind."

"Ms. Dong's opinion doesn't count."

"How's that?"

"She joined a non-Communist party and she used to study in the US. She was always sidelined."

"Is she now?"

"The Workers' Propaganda Team doesn't think highly of her."

"Don't look smart. With Mr. Jin in the hospital, who else can the Workers' Propaganda Team turn to?"

"We're going to elect a job assignment taskforce very soon."

"Who'll be on this taskforce? Students? Bah! They are just for show."

Although I agreed with Grandpa on this particular point, I would rather die than acknowledge the significance of Ms. Dong.

"The Workers' Propaganda Team will still ask Mr. Jin first. He can speak to them from his hospital bed."

Grandpa meditated, stroking his goatee.

"Some students in the opposite faction went to see Mr. Jin today. They are the shrewdest in the class. Why do you think they sucked up to him?"

"It's wrong to tell him to ignore Mr. Jin. Social climbers are hateful," Grandma chipped in. "You should be nice to people, not only because you need help. Mr. Jin will hate him."

"I didn't tell him to ignore Mr. Jin," Grandpa retorted. "According to Chairman Mao, everything has two sides. Both teachers are important. Our grandson was being loyal to Mr. Jin only. 'Mr. Jin and I belong to the same faction.' 'Mr. Jin and I get along well.' 'Ms. Dong's opinion doesn't count.' You must be nice to people, especially those people you have a grudge against. Our grandson is just too simple-minded! Remember these old sayings: 'Don't harm others, but beware of harm from others.' 'Be respectful and be on guard at the same time.' 'Keep your thoughts to yourself.'"

Grandma cut in, "You're preaching to deaf ears." On hindsight, how right she was!

Mom returned from a meeting at her shop just in time. After hearing a lengthy recap, she told Grandpa, "Let him be, Dad. Giving gifts is really not proper nowadays. There are policies about job assignments. Just relax."

The next morning, when Mom went to work and Grandma was washing vegetables downstairs, Grandpa sneaked over to my bedside to nudge me awake. Having tossed and turned in bed half the night, I was still drowsy then. However the stack of bank notes in his hand, mostly of one, two, or five jiao denominations, woke me up immediately.

Before I could roll out of bed, he had slipped them into my palm, whispering, "Take them." I pushed them away and he pushed them right back, gnashing his gums. All his teeth had fallen out but he refused to wear dentures, claiming that they would damage his appetite. In fact he was no gourmet at all. Liquor saturated bran dough, raw bean curd seasoned with sesame oil and salt, shrimp paste, and peanut butter made him a contented man. His favorite dish was crispy beans, stir-fried with pickles. When I think back on it, I guess he might have been wary of the cost of false teeth. Every month he was allowed to keep 9.6 jiao of his pension to himself to pay for cigarettes, tea leaves, haircuts, his Promethazine inhaler, an occasional ice cream or two for the kids, and so on. God knows how long it took him to save the money, around ten yuan in total, that he tried to squeeze into my hand. As we tussled, he broke his right little fingernail. I got some cotton fiber in my palm, since he kept his savings under the cotton batting of his bed all year round.

He was about to raise his voice when the thump of Grandma's bound feet approached the door. After casting me a glare, he stuffed the pile of bank notes back under the cotton batting.

At lunch break that day, the moment I entered the row of doors, wooden and inlaid with ground glass, that separated our room into two, I saw my grandparents seated on either side of a table near the window. Since the light came from behind them, it was hard to tell their facial expressions, but I sensed something extraordinary in their posture. More than anything else, it was the fact that Grandma was resting both hands on knees pulled close together, the tips of her bound feet touching the floor, a posture only seen in old family portraits. When I was three steps away from them, Grandpa spoke, "You're back."

"I'm back."

"Where were you this morning? At school?"

"Yes. I was at school. Honestly. What happened?"

"The notice has arrived."

His flat tone of voice triggered a click in my head.

The strange clicking haunted me for the next two or three years. It would be switched on as I walked around. It went faster as I picked up pace and stopped when I came to a dead stop. It sounded like knuckles cracking or a string of beads banging onto bones relentlessly. I was scared. Had I gone nuts? Would it eventually develop into dementia or paralysis, either of which was as good as being dead? Luckily the clicking went away eventually. Nonetheless it taught me a lesson: When caught off guard, never hold your breath and try to use your brain to control your body. The brain is an organ for fantasy not for effort.

On that particular day, at the click in my head, my soul detached itself from my body. It floated in the air watching my body function. First it saw my eye muscles pull the eyeballs to and fro over the notice. Actually the word "farm" alone told me everything I needed to know. All the other characters were just skimble-skamble. While satisfied with the performance of the eye muscles, my soul bore some grudge against my tear glands, which should at least have secreted some liquid. A teardrop the size of a soybean, hanging perilously on the corner of the eye, would be perfect. Tears streaming down the cheeks would be overdone, while dry eyes could hardly signal a surge of emotions. My mind was in turmoil! Disappointed with the tear glands, my soul shifted its attention to my Adam's apple expectantly. It was moving up and down, once, twice, three times! Great! Open your mouth, tighten your vocal cords, pause a few seconds—and then utter a sound. Your voice should quiver, your intonation should be rapid-fire, and your breath should be audible. Well done! Tighten your grip. Now you can rumple the notice, but don't ruin it ...

For the first time in my life I was divided into two—one being the director and the other, an actor. For the first time I realized that there was a role for me to play in life and an emotion to demonstrate. I wonder if others have had such an experience, or maybe it was just proof of my artistic talent. Anyway this show launched me into a new stage of life. I woke up to the reality that I had to conduct myself in conformity with societal expectations. Having emerged from the back stage onto the front stage, I was no longer who I was, but who I played. People would not judge me by my natural colors but by my persona. Of course, my "awakening" was only verbalized much later. Then and there, I had no other choice but to go with a blind force. Then and there, only two reactions stirred in my consciousness: One, am I going away from home? Two, will Grandpa scold me and sneer at me? Is it what I deserve after so many visits to Mr. Jin? However I decided against revealing such reactions because neither was normal. A normal reaction should be triggered by the fact that I had been assigned to work on a farm. But I simply failed to react to this fact. What should the normal reaction be? I wanted earnestly to know my grandparents' attitude, but their posture was already a put-up front against probing. They had recovered from the initial shock. I had missed the chance. As I sauntered on campus speculating on our job prospects with fellow students, the notice had been mailed to our home. That being the fact, whatever view I was to express, as long as it was different from theirs, would appear childish and ignorant. They would be let down. There was no way for them to share my view. Therefore my only way out was to flush out their position and cover my weak spots.

My soul heard myself yell, "What the f--k! I must find out. I'll raise hell ..."

Seeing a twitch at the corner of Grandpa's mouth, I went on alert at once, gasping and summoning my tears, just in case he had some harsh words ready.

He smiled, saying, "Eat your supper. What's done is done. We'll see afterward."

I didn't move.

Grandma chimed in, "Eat your supper. It's late. Aren't you hungry?"

I did some mental calculation. Was it proper now to switch from anger to submission?

Grandpa admonished, "Count yourself lucky! I was so worried. Chongming is a good place to go! It's still part of Shanghai, although on the wrong side of the river. Thank the Goddess of Mercy! We can still keep an eye on you. With your wage you won't starve. Don't go mad, just keep in mind there is a long way to go. We can't take care of you all your life. We're relieved that you have a place to go to."

Grandma said, "Well, everything goes back to where it started. You have a hard lot. Maybe one day luck will turn. Think about General Xue Rengui in the Tang dynasty. He had to leave his wife in a dilapidated cave dwelling to seek fame and fortune. There was no point getting stuck here, anyway."

"Right!" Grandpa addressed me affectionately. "Grandpa has thought it through for you. This is good. A blessing in disguise. Go there, find yourself a wife and settle down. Isn't this encouraged from the top? Make your home in Chongming. You have to marry late in Shanghai, but nobody cares in the countryside. Listen to your grandpa. How I wish to hold your son in my arms."

"When your son is born, Grandma will come to stay with you and take good care of him."

"After your marriage we will both join you in the countryside. The air is fresher and we can live on vegetables."

"Your grandpa is happy with bean curd for his meals. And I will become a vegetarian."

"Off you go. Find yourself a girl and get married. That's what Chairman Mao means by turning bad things into good things."

"Off you go! Be a man. Come, eat your supper."

The turn of conversation was so embarrassingly different from my expectation that I didn't know what to do with my facial muscles. Neither did my soul, the director of the show, know how to keep it going. My younger sister giggled. I stared at her before cracking a smile. There was no point in putting on a long face. However what had been make-believe became true. I had lost my appetite. The mailman must have arrived at 9 a.m. at the earliest. How had both my grandparents acquired such sanguinity in less than three hours? Why didn't they even try to show how sorry they were to let me go?

I saw immediately that they had no other alternative. Something had happened in our family. My mother had remarried. Although the mutual understanding was to keep the two families separate, and make no changes in the respective household registration booklets, and although the new guy had no say over whether I should leave or stay, my grandparents would have to let me go.

I found myself in the shoes of the powerful leader and strategist Cao Cao in the great classical novel, *Romance of Three Kingdoms*. He should have expected the burning of his warships at Chibi but he didn't. Likewise I should have anticipated this but I didn't.

I was not without a grudge. Why hadn't they told me so earlier? I could have written an application in my own blood to live and work in the Jinggang Mountains (Jiangxi province), the cradle of the Communist Revolution. My picture would appear in newspapers and the chief of the Municipal Revolutionary Committee would see me off. I could have become famous.

IV

The following days flashed by like a burst of light. I guess a person falling from a tall building would have similar feelings. Only one event left an indelible impression. It was about my clothing subsidy. Xiao Zhou, a pale-faced twenty-something on the school job assignment taskforce, pouted at me after rifling through the roster.

"You don't have it."

"Why don't I have it?"

"Don't you know?"

My heart sank. It must be my biological father again! Had it been futile for me to contradict classmates of the Five Red Categories, those from politically-preferred class backgrounds, who brandished their belt buckles at me? Or to make petition after petition to the Letters and Visits Offices of the Municipality, the People's Commune and the Municipal Revolutionary Committee? Or to bend over backward to join the Red Guards?

"I need an explanation." I grabbed him. "Tell me why."

"What?" Xiao Zhou glared. "Are you making a scene? Don't bluster just because you've got the notice. I still have your file. Under the dictatorship of the proletariat, I could cancel your job assignment with a phone call."

"Go ahead and cancel it!" My tear glands suddenly functioned. Scalding tears poured out. Tears that hadn't answered my beckoning on the day the notice arrived materialized in double strength. I must turn off the tap. I must not cry before a man with a face as white as that of the folk deity White *Wuchang*, messenger from hell. Otherwise I would be scandalized overnight. Who knew what dirty tricks those mean classmates of mine would play on me! However the tap refused to be turned off and my tears grew from trickles into torrents. Several other teachers on the job assignment taskforce peered over from five or six meters away. We were at the former Dean's Office. There was a ping pong table in the middle of the room, which had a floor area of more than one hundred square meters. Faculty meetings used to be convened around this table. Writing desks were arranged in the cubicles in the hallway beyond the threshold. The Workers' Propaganda Team didn't change the layout when they took over. They simply replaced some posters and staff.

With teary eyes I caught a vague glimpse of Mr. Yu, my Geometry teacher, Mr. Yang, my Geography teacher, and Mr. Niu, my Biology teacher, who were all hovering near the threshold regarding me. They had all spoken highly of my potential in public. How disappointed they would be seeing me cry like a girl!

Shame reduced me to broken utterances. "If you, you, don't explain, I, I won't leave … I won't go to Chongming!"

"Suit yourself. And don't blame anyone else." Xiao Zhou turned to leave.

I immediately dried my eyes and ran home to vent my grievances. Grandpa stood up and paced around the room. Then he told Grandma, "Go to his school. They have gone too far! If they're unreasonable, our grandson should really not go to Chongming. He can live on me. My pension is about twenty-six yuan per month, enough to support him. We've raised him to the age of nineteen. We could do more. After my death he'll figure out something else. The Communist Party has vowed to eliminate poverty. No one starves to death in a socialist country."

He made Grandma dress for the outing. He never ventured out of his home to attend to any family affair, be it a visit to a relative or a parent-teacher meeting. Meanwhile my mother was preoccupied with work. As a result Grandma acted as the family ambassador. She changed into a blue cloth smock with buttons on the right and a pair of dark black sultan pants, her one and only outfit for important occasions all year round. Although she made up her mind and got rid of the chignon she had worn for decades when the Cultural Revolution started, she stuck to the same hair smoother. I stood entranced, watching her carry the old fashioned black lacquered vanity box to the end table, put up the lid, and smooth her hair in front of the yellowed square of a mirror attached inside it.

Catching me in the mirror, Grandma asked, "What is the stare for?"

I blushed and dodged her eyes. I had never noticed previously how elegant she was when she combed her hair. Before leaving, Grandma tucked a man's hemp handkerchief into the front of her smock where the cloth buttons were. Even if it looked out of place to me, I knew better than to criticize.

It was twenty minutes' walk for me between home and school, but at least thirty minutes for Grandma with her bound feet. The clock had struck ten. The morning was almost over. When we were about two thirds through, Grandma suddenly said she needed a rest. We were in front of Xinhua Bookstore's Shanghai sales office on Middle Sichuan Road. The building, with smart granite steps and flower beds, used to house a foreign firm in pre-liberation China. On our way home from school, my classmates and I used to hang out on the edge of a flower bed, our feet dangling, watching how the window panes of the building opposite caught the setting sun, and savoring our freedom before returning home.

Grandma could certainly not climb onto the flower beds. She just sat on the steps. I stood by her wondering why she needed a rest. Hadn't she claimed that she could carry a basketful of food all the way from the fishmongers' to the wet market on Beijing Road and then to another wet market on Ningbo Road before finally making it home? That distance was by no means shorter than the one between home and my school. I rubbed my palm against the rough granite wall. The itchy ache was so addictive that I repeated the motion. In my mind's eye I saw tiny beads of blood burst out as my palm touched the wall. They swirled like a cyclone in red, triggering wave after wave of burning sensation inside me. A story that I had heard long before popped into my mind. An elementary school student struck down a mugger with only two fingers, an attainment he had been able to achieve by poking bricks on his way between home and school everyday. How easy it was! What a pity that my fingers had remained idle all the time. If I had his fingers, the pale-faced guy on the job assignment taskforce would have begged for mercy. If only the pain in my palm could dull the humiliation he had inflicted on me!

Grandma called out my name. I turned toward her, balling up my wounded palm. She was looking up at me, her high forehead shining in the midday sun, crow's feet fanning out from the corners of her squinting eyes. She regarded me as if either she were on her sick bed or I were behind bars.

"Let's call it quits, okay?" she asked. I noticed her pale purple lips. Had they always been purple or had they turned color just now? "Forget about it. Let's go home. We'll find some other way to make up for the clothing subsidy. The situation is bad enough. We'd better take the insult and not confront them. At my age I don't want heartburn from anger. I may die of it but life goes on for them. Let me live a couple more years to save you some trouble. With us alive in Shanghai, you can always come back if anything happens to you in the countryside. Snap out of it and go home! Dignity is as important to a person as bark is to a tree." She uttered the last words from clenched teeth. Unlike Grandpa, she had good teeth until her death. You should really have seen how her neat white teeth attacked shells or bones.

Grandma stood up and dusted her trouser bottoms. Strength had deserted me but I couldn't appear weak. I moved my wobbly legs. After a few steps I couldn't help but look back at the building.

I had just come of age on its steps under the colonnade. It was surely grand enough for such an important occasion in my life. Two naked giants with curly hair, probably figures from Greek mythology, used to protrude from the wall. They had risen up eight to nine meters to support the roof, and muscles were visible along their arms, legs, chests and abdomens. When the Cultural Revolution started, the moderates covered up their penises, and the radicals knocked down their torsos. A building deprived of giants, what a nice analogy for my fate!

V

"Hong Liu had dropped by," Grandpa reported.

"Hong Liu dropped by? Why? What did he say?"

"He was also assigned to Chongming," Grandma explained. "He came to see you."

"Was he? He's the eldest son in his family, too. And was he really assigned to Chongming like I was? How did he know about my assignment?"

"His mom came for a sanitary inspection yesterday. She is a nurse at the neighborhood clinic. She knew who I was, but I didn't know her. She introduced herself as Hong Liu's mom, and then I saw they did look alike. She said Hong Liu was on the School Revolutionary Committee, but a junior member only. That was why he got assigned to Chongming."

"Was he on the School Revolutionary Committee?"

"Seems so. A junior leader anyway."

Hey, how did he manage that?

"He said he would come again."

"Why didn't he tell me yesterday? I'll go find him."

"What's the rush about?" Grandpa asked. "Is it big enough to get you all excited?"

I rushed out of the house, ignoring him. He was prejudiced against Hong Liu because Hong Liu was too shrewd for his age. He had gotten that impression from me, and I had gotten it from the other students back in elementary school. Shrewd or not, he paid me a visit, even if he had joined the leadership. Where do you find friends like that?

It was only one and a half minutes' walk between my home and his building. Climbing up the forty-four terrazzo steps to his apartment on the third floor would take another minute and a half. I searched my memory, standing in front of his building. Wow! I hadn't been to his home for more than two years! Ashamed, I decided to climb the steps instead of yelling his name for him to come downstairs. He lived in one of the shabbiest pre-liberation buildings. Actually it had been converted into a residential quarters because it was too shabby for an office complex. It didn't even have an elevator. Other residential buildings dating back to the pre-liberation era had at least bare elevator shafts to remind people of their grander past.

Nevertheless, residents in such buildings looked down upon us *shikumen* residents. Hong Liu and I had once fought over the issue. He dismissed the odor of chamber pots in our rooms, and I countered by pointing out how desperate it would be for a diarrhea patient to live in his building and share the toilet with all other residents on the same floor. He ridiculed our lousy, dirty coal briquette stoves, and I warned him against being poisoned by gas ranges. He boasted of their rooftop terrace as a nice place to eat outdoors and enjoy the cool. I said our room was big enough to eat in and cool enough even in summer. He said that not all *shikumen* rooms were as big as ours, and that some were just pigeonholes. I pointed out how impractical it was for his family to pay similar rent to ours while occupying a space half the size.

He was so piqued by the last comment, not in the least because he had leaked the information to me himself, that he hit me by surprise. Unfortunately he sent my eyeglasses clanging to the cement floor. The glasses remained intact but the frame was broken in the middle. Before the glasses hit the floor he had vanished from my blurry sight. I asked for an adhesive bandage from a classmate living nearby to stick the frame back together.

After securing it on the bridge of my nose, I headed to his home for damages. He ran away as soon as he saw me at the foot of their staircase. I chased after him up the staircase and then down the fire escape. Eventually I gave up and decided to wait for his parents at their door.

After a while, he poked his head brazenly from the fire escape facing their door. I ignored him. He came down the fire escape gingerly, gesturing with two fingers, "Pause and break!" I pressed the bandage without saying a word. He descended further until he reached the last step. I hurled myself at him. He didn't dodge me. Instead he raised two fingers above his head like a weather vane on top of a house. His smile was so big that I was sure I could stuff an entire pancake into his mouth.

"Pause and break!"

I was so spellbound by the huge opening that my hand dropped to my side without touching him.

"Let's make peace." He stretched out his right hand. Surprised, I let him hold my right hand without thinking.

"It's celluloid, just plastic. I know how to fix it. Let's make peace."

"Fix my glasses or get me a new pair."

"I'll fix it right away. Can we be friends again?"

I didn't reply.

"It's my fault. But you shouldn't use the F-word either."

"When the hell did I use it?"

"You did. You said, 'F--k, it's so expensive to live in your building.'"

I was puzzled. I couldn't recall if I had actually used the word or not. If yes, then it was serious, because both my grandparents and mother demanded adamantly that I rid my speech of such indecency. The same went for his parents. We had agreed to help each other mind our language to avoid ear boxing and head slapping. If our parents met to discuss damages, Hong Liu could ruin me by mentioning the F-word.

"Let's make peace." He shook my hand again.

"Okay," I said, "but you have to fix my glasses."

"No problem," he answered happily, fishing out a key to their apartment. His solution was to strike a match, hold the frame over it, and pinch the two parts together when the plastic was about to melt. He took care of the match, and I, the frame. He claimed he had fixed his own glasses this way, but judging by our progress I highly doubted it. Despite the pile of used matches and the bad smell of burning plastic, the frame remained broken. He then decided to strike several matches simultaneously. At long last, when we had almost run out of matches, the frame came together. However the blackish ridge where the two pieces joined was anything but unnoticeable. Hong Liu told me to wait until the next day to wear my glasses, because by then the melted plastic would solidify.

I fumbled my way home, but sometime before getting inside I slipped the glasses back on. Grandpa demanded an explanation. I said I had broken them by accident, but they had been fixed. In order to prove my point I moved my cheeks. Little did I expect them to break again. Feeling the fragments against my temples, I regretted not having listened to Hong Liu and wasting two hours plus an entire box of matches. Despite their grumbles I got a new frame. Several days later, my grandparents interrogated me again because they had heard about it from a classmate. I had no choice but to relate the entire story, except for the F-word.

Grandpa poked my head with his fingernail, "Why aren't you as clever as he is? As the old saying goes: 'A fall into the pit, a gain in your wit.' Learn from this. Stay away from people who think of themselves first."

I thought to myself, "You think he is sharp because you don't know about the F-word." I felt I was the clever one, because as perceptive as Grandpa was, I had fooled him.

As I reminisced at Hong Liu's building, my trouser leg swept over a cardboard box and then I tripped over an empty tin can. Clang, clang, the tin can rolled down the long narrow hallway intended for offices. Cobwebs covered holes where ceiling lamps used to be. With gas ranges and miscellaneous items placed haphazardly outside doors, this hallway was full of booby traps. My vision should have been okay because it had been conditioned by the even darker stairway in our *shikumen* house, but I had let my mind wander. Someone cursed loudly at the clanging. I was secretly happy. "A small bump heralds the smooth road ahead." If you recited this sentence three times after making a minor mistake, things would get straightened out of their own accord. A tip I had obtained recently on how to master one's own fate.

Hong Liu was not at home. His parents didn't even know about his visit to my house. "Oh, has he been to your place already?" his mother remarked. "What good buddies you are. Now that your paths are crossing again, try to look out for each other out there in Chongming." How gratifying it was to find a person who appreciated me.

His father presented me with a cup of tea. Through the yellowish orange water I saw that the tea leaves were piled in, taking up one third of the cup. I was touched. He was the first person to treat me as an adult and a guest. I received the cup with both hands, a protocol Grandpa had instilled in me. Then I sat straight in my seat like Grandpa had taught me.

Hong Liu's father asked, "I haven't seen you at the community green for a while. Where do you practice now?"

"The job assignment thing gets in the way. I can't concentrate."

"Right. Right." His father nodded. As a matter of fact, his father and I had been practicing the same style of Chinese boxing, the 88 Yang-Style *Taiji* Moves, at the same community green at the corner of Fuzhou Road and Hubei Road. Our masters were old friends and rivals of equal strength in the partner-based discipline of *Taiji* Push Hands. We had been formally inducted at around the same time in late 1967, when *taiji* boxing was no longer banned in public. However I had made more progress than he had. By now I could resist his master for about ten minutes in Push Hands, whereas he, according to his master, had yet to open up his joints. His master said, in order to practice *taiji* boxing well, one had to open up one's joints so that both *qi* and blood could flow freely. With that he gave us a demonstration by cracking his two shoulder blades like clappers. Because they were the most difficult to crack, if you could crack them, you could crack any other bones. By now I had practiced enough to generate a click in my left shoulder blade, audible to my own ears only, whereas Hong Liu's father had never been able to do it. Relaxed at that thought, I took a sip of the tea.

Hong Liu's father and I were still discussing *taiji* boxing when Hong Liu returned. He immediately waved his right index finger at me, the way the neighborhood administrator swung a bell to call on residents to do a clean-up. "Haha, it's you! What in the world? We just can't see enough of each other. I went to your place. Did you know?"

He looked different at first sight. Then I realized his eyeglasses were missing. Eyeglasses had been the bond between us in primary school, because we were the only two students in our class wearing them. However he had always stressed how different we were from each other: He had inherited poor vision from his mother while I had ruined my own eyesight. God knows why he had removed his glasses, without which he could hardly see anything two years before. Now his eyes were bulging like the eyes of a toad, and his previously feminine oval face was tanned in a masculine manner. The pity was he had not grown taller. Regardless, I thought he looked like a leader.

Half a year later, I found out why he had removed his eyeglasses. He had been in love. It was the power of Cupid, not Mars.

"What a silver lining!" He stood in front of my chair. "We'll be on the same farm. All the high school graduates from the same district in Shanghai are assigned to the same farm. We must keep in touch. I've made all sorts of friends in the past two years. I'll introduce them to you and you to them. One relies on parents when at home and on friends when outside. We must help each other. All these movements at school these past two years kept me away from books. It will be different on the farm. I will read and keep fit. We must talk to each other often. I'm serious. You're the only friend I can discuss books with. Do you plan to study too?"

I nodded although I hadn't thought about it. My only concern so far was the rumor that thugs reigned on the farms in Chongming. Thugs scared me more than ghosts. Those mean classmates of mine had been giving me a rough time the past ten years, but they were a far cry from thugs. I was not going to eat dirt on the farm. A scholar is always wrong in front of a gunman. That was why I was taking some cram courses of Eight Diagram Boxing at the community green, although I was not optimistic about the outcome. Hong Liu's emphasis on study comforted me a lot.

Hong Liu saw I was distracted. "Hello? Don't you believe me? I'm serious. I'll study. I'll bring nothing but books to the farm. No food whatsoever. I tried to make you leave your schoolbooks and join the movements, but now I see you were the practical one. How far have you progressed?"

"I think I'm done with high school algebra. That's it." I shut my mouth before another sentence, "But I don't recall anything," slipped out.

"Super!" he cried out. His voice was much louder than before. His hands grabbed at the air, his ulna and tendons visible under the skin, which reminded me of an incident two years before, with a yellowing coverless book on the desk in front of me. Not quite as big as a standard paperback, it was his treasured public speaking guide. There were illustrations of gestures useful for public speaking. I still remembered some of them. If a speaker raises his right hand, points the index finger at the sky, and focuses both eyes somehow on the tip of the index finger, he is gesturing, "Listen to me, please." If a speaker leans forward, puts his right hand across his chest, and points his right fingers at his body an inch or so below the hollow of his left shoulder—the way posters depicted Lenin making a speech at Red Square in Moscow—he is indicating, "I believe." If a speaker extends his right arm as far backward as possible and tilts his head to the left, forming a straight line between the back of his head and his right index finger, he means, "Don't listen to him." When I dropped in on Hong Liu the previous time, he was practicing those gestures repeatedlyin front of the mirror. His puppet-like motions were so funny that I still remembered them after two years. Now he seemed to have internalized them. I was secretly impressed.

We had become good friends because we found merits in each other. While I was keeping my regard secret, he was putting his admiration for me in words, "When can you show me the ropes? I want to self study high school textbooks too. You said a high school education is the minimum one needs. I can't agree with you more."

"That's what a famous scientist said. I remember his name was …"

"I'll attribute it to you anyway. You were a top student. You are smart. I really need your help. I'm so glad we're on the same farm. We must keep in touch. Don't lose heart. Your grandmother said you were unhappy. Don't be! The good thing about the farm is we'll have plenty of time to ourselves. If you work in a factory, you're busy from eight to five. It's true. I've asked around. Working on a farm may be bad for others but good for us."

Now I really looked at Hong Liu with new eyes. He was almost as philosophical as my grandpa. They'd both come to a true understanding of the dialectics of turning bad things into good things.

Hong Liu went on to tell me a story. Once upon a time, a man made a bet with a rich man that he could stay confined to a room for ten years as long as he had books to read (and food and water, of course). On the eve of the tenth anniversary, the rich man sent an assassin to kill him, only to find he had left. He propped a note on the desk, saying he had gained so much from reading over the past ten years that he decided to go without the money.

"Didn't you ever hear of the story?" Hong Liu sounded surprised. "It was written by Anton Chekhov."

Yes I knew Chekhov. I had read his *Vanka* in primary school and *The Chameleon* later. I also knew he was a progressive writer for the people, a member of the bourgeois critical realism school. He was critical of capitalism but saw no way out of it. There were only a few pieces of his work available, etc., etc. However I had no idea about this story, a famous one judging by Hong Liu's demeanor.

I then blurted out the most important decision so far in my life, or you might say the only voluntary decision. All other decisions had been made for me, and I was just a rubber stamp. This one was different. I acted on my own, and I was going to disrupt the unfolding of preordained destiny.

"I'll get myself transferred to your school. We'll leave together."

Hong Liu hesitated, but luckily his hesitation lasted no more than five seconds, because after five seconds, my self-esteem would have forced me to say, "Just kidding." If that happened, I would pretend this idea never existed, however sincere his apologies were. I knew my own disposition. Fortunately it didn't happen.

"Great. That's awesome!" He slapped my shoulder laughing. "Get yourself transferred. No problem at all."

"I ..." I recoiled at the slap. "Three other students in my class are assigned to the farm in Chongming. We don't get along. We belong to different factions ..." I played with the facts slightly, leveraging my reputation for never telling lies. It was true that three male students and one female student at my school were assigned to Chongming, but all three male students belonged to the same faction.

"No problem. No problem at all. Just go through the formalities."

"Is it okay to transfer?"

"Why shouldn't it be? You're still going, only to a different production team. If they don't let you transfer, you just refuse to go. Our school will take you in happily. I'm the head of our team to Chongming anyway."

"But it may be quite a pain …"

"It's no big deal. Do you want me to get the Workers' Propaganda Team at our school to talk to yours? We're on good terms."

"No. No." The nauseatingly pale-faced guy on the Workers' Propaganda Team at our school popped into my mind. Moreover I didn't want Hong Liu to consider me incompetent. We were going to be spending our lives together, maybe our entire life. He shouldn't patronize me.

My indecisiveness upset him. In fact I was hoping for a more enthusiastic second invitation from him. This was, after all, a major decision for me. Just like Zhuge Liang leaving his hermitage at the Wolonggang, this was a journey of no return. However Hong Liu had changed the subject. He asked me which books to bring, which books we could share, and of which books we must each have a copy. He thought we were done but I didn't think so.

I cut in when he paused to take a breath, "I'll think about it and let you know later."

"What? What more is there to think about?" he shouted, knitting his brows.

"This is huge. You must let him think," his mother intervened. "He has also to get advice from his parents."

"Why?" he sighed. "Why do we always need advice from parents? We've stepped into society now, and we need to make our own judgments. Otherwise what will we do in Chongming? Also, his grandparents and mother know me. There's nothing for them to worry about if you join our team, is there?"

Since he directed the last question at me, I nodded emphatically. This was exactly what I was not sure of.

To my surprise, Grandpa didn't lose his temper upon hearing

my decision. Hong Liu's assertiveness in front of his parents had impressed me deeply. According to *How to be a Good Communist*, Confucianism prioritized a gentleman's self-cultivation in the following order: cultivating one's moral character, putting one's family affairs in order, running the local government well, and bringing peace to the entire country. Therefore a person who wants to be respected by others must first win respect from his family. Since I was leaving in about ten days anyway, I might as well assert myself at home.

It was in vain. Grandpa lost neither his temper nor his calm. He sucked repeatedly at a cigarillo the length of a mahjong tile, before remarking knowingly, "Put away your little tricks."

His foresight was unnerving. To think I had prided myself on a "spontaneous" decision! He saw right through it.

The valor Hong Liu had instilled in me was gone. I resorted to the usual whining, "I don't get along with my classmates. Our team leader is from another faction. I've promised Hong Liu ..."

Grandpa didn't change his countenance. After I had whined enough he rested the cigarillo gingerly on the dent in the glass ashtray.

"You can join his team on one condition."

I was suddenly alert, as if someone had just poured a bucket of cold water over me. This condition must be no trivial matter.

"You'll get the worst of it if you hang out with people shrewder than you. Bear this in mind and don't complain."

I could hardly mask my disappointment. This was by no means an earth-shaking truth. Nevertheless my wish was granted. I was glad. I saw hope. I had earned a chance to cut off all previous complications and worries. I was going to make a fresh start out there in the world. To hell with all the grievances and humiliations!

VI

Since Hong Liu's team was scheduled to leave Shanghai a dozen days earlier than the team at my school, I had to hurry. Whenever I had free time I dropped in on him. I had to get to know him once more, because he had changed, otherwise he wouldn't have made it onto the school revolutionary committee. Busy as he was, he was not at home eight out of ten times I visited. When he finally came home, his face flushed by drinks, several other students followed and packed the room. He generously introduced these friends to me. Since none of them would go to Chongming, I didn't commit their names to memory.

Among those who would go to Chongming, some were said to be his best friends. One was Wang Mingquan. Because they shared a surname, he was nicknamed "Wang Jingwei," after the head of the regime established in 1940 to govern the Japanese-conquered territory in China. Sometimes he was simply called Jing. Another was a girl named Zheng Guomei, nicknamed "Hot Water Bottle" or "Commander Hot Water." Both were platoon leaders in the Red Guard and die-hard members of his faction. The three of them had vowed to be friends until death. Four years on the farm would teach me that anyone who made such vows was either a scoundrel or an idiot, but back then I admired them hugely. Hong Liu himself went by the nickname "Embroidered Pillow" or "Lacework" or simply "Lacey."

I refused to tell him my nickname at my middle school,

because shaking it off was one of the reasons why I decided to join his team. He laughed, saying "Smart Ass" was such a catchy nickname that he hoped to spread it with my permission. I was furious. Turning back the wheel of history should never be allowed. I warned him sternly against leaking my nickname to any fellow student or future colleague on the farm. If he couldn't keep secret I would leave him immediately. He laughed again and swore never to mention Smart Ass on any occasion, not even in his dreams. If he went back on his word I could slap him on the face ten times in public. Sounding very sincere, he said that he hated people being called by nicknames too, but lowbrow folks like catchy, memorable nicknames. They are not used to the idea of human dignity.

"You have to live with it or you risk isolation. That's what Chairman Mao meant by 'driving one's friends to the side of enemy.' Just don't take them seriously and have self-respect. Nicknames are merely symbols. So are names. Numbers such as one, two, three and four can also serve as names. Don't give a damn what they call you! The Nationalist Party used to call the Communist Party 'Communist bandits,' but Chairman Mao was so versed in military strategy that he eventually defeated Generalissimo Chiang. If you find nicknames disgusting, you could invent a nice one for yourself and make others adopt it. Overused nicknames lose their popularity the way over-boiled tea leaves lose their flavor."

I was still not convinced. Sure enough, I got a new nickname almost the moment I arrived at the farm. Thinking back on Hong Liu's advice, I somehow felt better.

Although Hong Liu promised over and again to take me to the homes of Jing and Commander Hot Water, or to introduce them to me at his place, so far we hadn't met. Apologetically Hong Liu introduced me to a bearded neighbor living in Building No. 4, whom he addressed as "Uncle." According to Hong Liu, Uncle was extraordinary. Adept with both the pen and the fist, brave and resourceful, Uncle had led a division of the Red Workers Rebel Command. Red Workers were day laborers. Uncle had been a longtime day laborer because he was so skilled at lathe and bench work and using a shave horse that he could seek employment wherever he wanted, at wages twice of those of regular workers. Hong Liu also learned that Uncle had rejected several employers' offers to become a full-time worker. However when the Cultural Revolution started, Uncle decided it was better to have a regular job so he joined the Red Workers Rebel Command.

After the "January Storm" in 1967, the Red Workers Rebel Command was disbanded as a profiteering organization. At the moment Uncle was out of job but he was not hard pressed, because he had a great wife who not only brought home a decent wage as a loom tender at a woolen mill but also saw to the housework. He was the man of the house, enjoying nice dishes with drinks every meal. Hong Liu was deeply impressed. Moreover Uncle was a renowned chess player and street fighter. His friends were even more awesome. There was Mr. Niu, who played the musical saw, the only person I knew who could. Also a Mr. Pi, who had learned the Eight Diagram Boxing from a monk at the Wudang Mountains (Hubei province) so well that he had once broken a column with a single blow. But these days he would rather get slapped on the face than hit others, probably because he knew too well the strength of his fists. Mr. Niu admired Mr. Pi. So after seeing Mr. Niu play the musical saw, Hong Liu became a fan of Mr. Pi's without meeting the latter in person.

Hong Liu found time in his busy schedule to spend with Uncle so as to gain some street smarts. He said Jing and some of the others were also intimate with Uncle and thought highly of him. The first time I went over to Uncle's place, he invited me to play chess with him. I declined because I didn't want to make a fool of myself. Uncle said that in the past, every person who called himself a scholar was a master of painting, calligraphy, music and chess. He also said a game of chess revealed a lot about character. In order to prove my character, I agreed to play against him. Since

I had the black pieces I opened the first game. Throughout the game I followed the great master Wang Jialiang's chess manual. I made a clean sweep. Not realizing he had lost to Wang Jialiang, Uncle changed his countenance and muttered, "Never once in twenty years' time. I must concentrate." He opened the second game. After about ten moves I maneuvered pieces as suggested by Tu Jingming's *Introduction to Chess Opening.* I won again. Hong Liu started to drop hints to me. To be frank, I had no more tricks up my sleeves. Yet Uncle was such a paper tiger that during the third game, he didn't even dare to move his pieces across the border to challenge mine. We ended up in a draw, much to his relief.

His wife lost no time in serving lunch. He offered me a drink. I hastened to confess that I didn't drink. Hong Liu testified for me. Uncle took a close look at my forehead, saying, "What a smart boy. I've never seen anyone smarter. You're bound to go far. Hong Liu, don't be angry with me. Your classmate here will achieve greater things than you. You've made the right friend."

When we left, Hong Liu turned to me. "How are you feeling now? Much better? I said you'd be all right. I've always said so. Uncle agrees with me. Of all my friends and classmates, he singled you out. There, there, rest assured. You might have lost touch because you didn't participate in the movements. But don't worry. One picks up things like that really quickly. You must know this already from reading Balzac's novels. What? You haven't read them? I'll find some for you later. Once you read them, you'll see. It's really easy. Trust me. Hanging out with people like Uncle is only the first step. We're meant for big things. When you become a big guy, remember me."

The more he talked, the more I felt it necessary to keep Wang Jialiang and Tu Jingming to myself. I should definitely acquire more skills because you never knew when they would come in handy. Well, I had another chess manual by Yang Guanlin. I should study it and then impress Uncle one more time.

However, back at home, I was too excited to study the chess

manual. Instead I cooked up a poem entitled *For a Friend on the Eve of Departing for Chongming* that didn't exactly rhyme. The second stanza read: "We shared our ambitions as we strolled, they will come true if we have the will. Snow made the road ahead muddy, but it may turn into spring showers any time." I transcribed the poem with a writing brush, planning it as a gift for Hong Liu. Little did I expect that he and I would part ways before it reached his hand.

VII

Other than dropping in on Hong Liu, I busied myself with packing.

My luggage was minimal. As a result I remember all the items to this day. There was a leather trunk. Genuine leather, mind you, not synthetic. But it had grown brittle with age because it dated back to the days when Grandpa fled from the invading Japanese troops. Thanks to the loops of straw rope that fastened it, the trunk arrived at the farm safe and sound. Inside the trunk there was a blue cloth liner. A crescent pocket with pretty folds was sewn to the liner inside the lid. In it were my valuables: a ten yuan bill; five grain coupons, acknowledged nationwide, worth 1.5 kilograms each; a bar of soap; a box of matches; and a large sewing kit that Grandma had made from some brown corduroy. During the packing stage we heard that soap and matches were in short supply in the countryside. Once on the farm, I realized it was hearsay. The farm shop might run out of other goods, but never soap or matches, which was powerful proof that Chongming was part of Shanghai and on the verge of Paradise. However rumor had it that Chongming was to be returned to the jurisdiction of Jiangsu province. Therefore I dared not actually use my soap and matches from Shanghai. By and by they became a fixture in my trunk, the way the Monkey King's golden cudgel had stayed at the Dragon King's Palace. Four years later, when I left the farm to work in Shanghai, I kept them in the pocket in memory of a part of my bygone life. The trunk was checked on my journey back anyway.

The grain coupons were intended for my evacuation from Chongming via Haimen, in case war broke out and the waterway between Shanghai and Chongming was cut off. As war always loomed on the horizon, I didn't dare to exchange them for a chicken. Back then one could trade grain coupons worth 7.5 kilograms for a decent chicken. As for the ten yuan bill, you know what it was for. Later I read in *A Biography of Tanaka Kakuei* that when the future Prime Minister of Japan first left home to seek a living, his mother told him a man must always have ten yen with him. That made me on an equal footing with a Prime Minister. Fantastic! Finding qualities great people and I shared was a main driver behind my interest in celebrity biographies.

It goes without saying that the sewing kit was the most useful on the farm.

Of all my clothes, only three were unpatched. The first one was a blue twilled-cotton Mao suit inherited from my grandmother's brother, who had died of gastric cancer. Since cancer was not contagious, Grandma took his suit. Grandpa had worn it several times, but standing at less than 170 centimeters, he was too small for a suit of someone who was 180 centimeters tall. Although Grandpa was not particular about clothes, the suit made him shrink. Moreover Grandpa had never gotten used to Mao suits. Grandma saved it in a trunk with mothballs for me to grow up into, even if I was only around 140 centimeters tall at that time. Now I stood at barely 165 centimeters. Grandma had no choice but to shorten the sleeves and hem the pants so that I had at least one presentable outfit on the farm. She didn't shorten them much, though, because she believed I could still grow. When I disappointed her, she blamed it on the loads I carried on a shoulder pole at the farm.

The second item was a set of fine canvas work fatigues handed down by my mother's new husband. A few years later when their relationship went sour, he made a detailed list of things given to my mother, but he forgot this very important item. In the more than ten years' time during which we were related, these fatigues seem to be the only thing I got from him. Maybe there were a few packets of biscuits but I lost track. However as the saying goes: "The favor of a drop of water should be rewarded with a fountain." I shouldn't understate its value. It was the outfit I wore the most on the farm and the most durable. In it I could move whichever way I wanted. Tattered clothes made the wearer nervous, as did brand new clothes because they might easily tear on the back or at the elbows, especially when the wearer was sweating. I knew this only too well. The fatigues were different. Despite the fact that eventually patches were placed on the back and elbows, it was so sturdy that I wore it with confidence.

The outfit had originally been navy blue but was a frayed pale blue when it came into my possession. I made Grandma dye it brown so that dirt wouldn't show. In addition I had her alter it into a jacket by replacing some buttons with a zipper, adding two slant sandwich pockets, and attaching an inch-wide elastic band to the lower hem, because I thought fatigues were out. Nevertheless the slogan across the left chest that read "Safety in Production" remained indelible. I had some misgivings about it for quite some time before realizing that it was actually the most valuable part of the clothes. Back then, no other outfit, however neat or fashionable (suits and ties were off limits), could top wrinkled work fatigues with "Safety in Production" printed across them. People roaming Shanghai's streets in neat clothes, such as woolen Mao suits, actually worked in the countryside, whereas those who draped themselves casually in work fatigues were true Shanghai residents. Young people in Shanghai eventually learned to prefer work fatigues to military uniforms. How I regretted having my fatigues dyed and altered.

Enough said about the work fatigues.

The third one was a more expensive short overcoat with plush lining. It had originally belonged to my mother, but had been altered for my biological father between 1957 and 1958 when they remarried. Around that time, blue twilled-cotton, double-breasted Lenin coats with camel hair lining were in vogue. My father suggested having it altered for him since my mother couldn't wear it anyway (in that coat, she would be ridiculed as a young bourgeois mistress of the house) and moths would feast on it. My mother agreed, about which my grandmother grumbled a lot, complaining that my mother lost her marbles when in love. After their second divorce, he didn't take it away. Ten years later, it was unearthed again for my sake. The blue outer layer was already rotting, and nobody wore double-breasted Lenin coats any longer. So we bought some off-white fine cloth, dyed it brown, and made a new shell. Although fine cloth was inferior to the original twilled-cotton, the plush lining was of good quality. The lining appeared shorter and stiffer than the new plush collar, but Grandma praised it for not shedding a single hair. I took a closer look at it. Indeed it was glossy despite its age. A person in such a coat could well pass for an impoverished aristocrat. In China, an impoverished aristocrat was criticized for squandering away the family wealth but respected for his blue blood. I felt it deeply when I wore the coat in winter.

I will skip over the other clothes, although Grandma, Mother and I did take great pains to mend them. Besides clothes, I packed books, an entire valise of books. Hong Liu's enthusiasm had infected me. I looked forward to some serious study on the farm in Chongming.

I had buried myself in books, something I took the greatest pride in later. The media, if they are ever interested in me, could cite this as evidence of my foresight. By October 1966, almost all Red Guards were on the road "exchanging revolutionary ideas," and the "Red Terror" had bored its own executors. I was likewise eager to see the beauty of China with my own eyes without worrying about expenses. My grandparents went all out to thwart my ambition, but they wouldn't have succeeded if I hadn't chickened out in the first place. Having had a hard time from the Red Guards, I couldn't help but become a coward, apprehensive of any challenge against my political background. Some good friends of mine, like Hong Liu and Xiong Shijie, had gone away without any warning, which broke my heart and made me lament the inconstancy of human relationships. In reality I wanted my grandparents to stop me, so that they became the scapegoats for my inaction. Apart from taking my younger brother to some literary and artistic groups, and colleges and universities in Shanghai, I had nothing better to do than to read. That leading figure of modern Chinese literature, Lu Xun, had seen it decades before: "Only bored people read."

I studied math, physics and chemistry for Junior Three and high school students. "A person knowledgeable about math, physics and chemistry can thrive anywhere on earth." Such a saying had been heavily criticized since 1964 so I was deeply impressed. We had conscientiously distanced ourselves from liberal arts subjects since we entered junior high school. A man should aspire to become a scientist or an engineer, while girls could dream about careers in medicine and education. Later, while on the farm, I switched to literature, and then stuck with it ever since, only because I came to see no way out by studying math, physics or chemistry. But back then, thinking that the College Entrance Examinations would be restored, I went at math, physics and chemistry relentlessly.

Mother borrowed relevant books for me from the library at the Municipal Workers' Cultural Hall. Shortly afterward, that library was closed for "clean-up and rectification," cutting off my book supply. There were similar books at the bookstore where Mother worked, but, as scrupulous in separating public from private interests as she was, she never borrowed any book that was for sale. The picture books and novels she borrowed for me were all from their staff library. The staff library didn't carry school textbooks, and it was closed in the end as well. Of course I could have bought those textbooks, but even a used textbook cost eight jiao or one yuan. What was the use of such books once you had done all the exercises in them and mastered the knowledge? Ever since fifth grade I had been saving a little money with every textbook by using secondhand ones, or substandard ones sold at reduced prices by the printer, even if they weren't available until a week after the start of a term. The inconvenience of borrowing from my deskmate was negligible. Consequently, to this day, I refrain from scribbling on my books so that their new owners, if there is such a possibility, won't find me too obnoxious. Another consequence is that I prefer copying out books to buying them, because it's very cost effective to reinforce one's memory and practice one's handwriting simultaneously.

A covert reason why I didn't ask my mother to buy books was that I was afraid I might give up halfway. I kept thinking about joining the movements and doubting whether it was wise to pursue academic competence to the neglect of political orientation. The *Algebra III* section of the *Math, Physics and Chemistry Self Study Series* that Mother borrowed from the library was left unfinished after two months. The return on investment in books was too painful to think about.

I found a place where I could read books for free. It was the salesroom of the China Book Traders at the corner of Henan Road and Fuzhou Road. An open-shelf policy was followed there even in 1966 and 1967. The books were put behind counters in the 1970s, but soon they were accessible again. It was simply a paradise for book lovers.

How I miss the serenity there!

Snow-white ceiling, flaming red terrazzo floor, cream-colored shelves, and a wide variety of books. The few people inside, no more than thirty including the sales clerks, dotted the hall like islands in a vast ocean. Nobody raised a voice or clattered around. No marches were played through the loudspeaker. No crowd gathered outside to beat gongs, sound drums or shout slogans. New arrivals felt as if they were walking into the shade on a hot summer day, sweet saliva welling up in their mouths, or lying on a beach after a swim in the sea, all pores open to the sensation of bliss. I avail of this opportunity to pay my belated tribute to those people who made such an oasis possible.

Naturally things become perfect only in reminiscence. Our brains remember selectively. Back then I was torn between ecstasy and dread, ecstasy at finding such a place, and dread that the sales clerks would shoo me out once they decided I was not going to buy anything. I put on a show of browsing different shelves before pulling out the real target, *Algebra III*. After turning a few pages, I looked around. Nobody was taking notice. I sidled away to lean against a glass-framed counter a meter from the shelf, and began to study the chapter I was interested in. In about fifteen minutes' time, I looked around, moved from the counter to the shelf, and went on with my study. In another quarter of an hour, I repeated the moves. When the closing bell rang after two hours, I had finished an entire chapter. The next day, with a pen and a self-made notebook in my trouser pocket, I pushed open the glass door confidently and headed directly for the shelf displaying *Algebra III*. Having tossed around in bed half the night, I came to the conclusion that acting natural was the best disguise. It wasn't until half an hour later, when I reached for my pen and notebook to solve a problem, that I became aware of someone staring. It was a big woman with a round face, a pair of round eyes, a plump neck and two plump arms. The claret-colored armband stretched over her arm read "Sales." Startled, I squeezed the book in on a shelf and made for the exit. After a few steps, there was a thundering voice behind me, "Come back here."

"Are you talking to me?"

"Come over here!"

"What? Why?"

"What have you done with the book?" The big woman raised the book in her hand. In my scramble to stuff it back, the bottom of the cover had been bent upward.

I protected my trouser pocket without thinking, scared that she was going to demand damages. In my thin plastic wallet, besides my student ID, there was only a five jiao bill, which I had been saving for three months.

"What's in your pocket?"

"Nothing."

"Take it out."

Blood rushed into my face when it dawned on me what she suspected. Nobody had ever accused me of shoplifting in my life. How dare she!

With a bang, I slapped my notebook, pen and plastic wallet onto the glass-framed counter. She picked up my notebook and looked.

"Oh. You brought this."

I grabbed it from her. I would have boxed her ears, if I had had the balls to challenge the wrath of the masses during the Cultural Revolution. With flesh like hers, my slap would go down resoundingly! I fantasized about it on my way home.

The next day I went to the bookstore again. If I didn't go I would prove myself a coward. She didn't own the store. Why couldn't I go?

She was right there by the shelf. She saw me. I hesitated. Was it worthwhile to get into a fight with a person like her?

"Come here!" she shouted at me. My calves shook uncontrollably. I went toward her despite them. She approached me at the same time. "You there, are you here to read?"

"Is it not allowed?"

"Don't talk back. Nobody wants to quarrel with you." The flesh on her plump face creased into a smile. "Book readers must be book lovers. If you damage a book, who are we going to sell it to?"

No discord, no concord. My status at the bookstore grew with each passing day, from spreading the book on a counter, to occupying a foot stool that sales clerks used to reach books on higher shelves, and then to sitting on a square stool, brought to me by the plump lady, and spreading the book on the counter in front of me. In over two months' time, I finished plane geometry plus high school algebra, and made some inroads into trigonometry. Romain Rolland once said something to the effect that you live a double life because you don't have much time to live. I doubled my reading exactly because I didn't have a good environment in which to read.

Before leaving for the countryside, I bought books like crazy, not only books I had resisted buying but also those I had read at the bookstore on Henan Road. Besides an entire set of *Self Study Series*, I also got hold of *Advanced Mathematics* by Fan Yingchuan, which was said to be superior to any other book on the subject. It came in two volumes and cost one yuan and one jiao secondhand. The supplementary workbook cost another one yuan and five jiao. I was determined to have them all. As for liberal arts books, I packed *Three Hundred Tang Poems* and *Poetic Patterns* by Zhou Zhenfu. Neither was likely to get me into trouble because Chairman Mao quoted Tang poems in his own work and Zhou Zhenfu annotated the Chairman's poetry. Then I added *Nine Editorials in Response to the Open Letter from the Central Committee of the Communist Party of the Soviet Union*, plus *On Hai Rui Dismissed from Office* by Yao Wenyuan. At the last moment I threw in *A General History of China* by Fan Wenlan and the great classical novel, *A Dream of Red Mansions*.

A dome-shaped mosquito net stood out in my luggage. It was indeed the only legacy from my biological father.

VIII

I hated my father.

I had hated him since childhood. The hatred continued until his death. I thought it would go on until I died.

I hated him because all my hatred for him was in vain. Despite my reiteration of how and why I hated him, my audiences were never convinced. They were exactly the ones who demanded that I make a clean break with him. When I did as told, they just wouldn't believe me. Some paid lip service to my sincerity, if they happened to be in a good mood, were on friendly terms with me, or had no interest in setting themselves against me, but the disbelief lingered. I had to go into each new environment or face each new group of people and repeat the process. Eventually I realized that my father to me was like Materialism to Lenin. As I recall, Lenin claimed that he had refuted Materialism a thousand times, but that he attacked it the 1,001st time nevertheless.

My father got me into a labyrinth where I always returned to the starting point in exhaustion. He was the labyrinth I had been born into. I knew little of him. Any coherent information about him had been passed on to me later by my grandparents and my mother. What I got firsthand from him were just some vague fragmented impressions. My younger siblings fared even worse. When my mother divorced him the first time, my younger sister was only a fetus. To her, he was merely a faceless specter. Of course she had seen him in person but I was sure she had no recollection at all. She saw him for the last time at the age of five. When I was five, my mother broke up with him the first time. Such a major event hadn't even left a dent in my memory. My initial impression of him was formed when I was six. Instead of living at home he stayed at the single dorm at his factory. However he visited us frequently, at least once a week. When he came he would sit there, either striking up a conversation or remaining quiet. He didn't talk much; maybe it was the circumstances at home, or his personality, or it was just my impression. There is no way to ascertain now.

We tried not to discuss him unless we had to. Without the Red Guards I would have known even less of him. It was always awkward discussing him. For one thing, what was the appropriate way to refer to him? My grandparents used his name. My mother had a particular look when she had to talk about him. As for us children, we resorted to "he," "him" or "that person" because the grownups didn't allow us to mention his name or the term "Father." "He" made our tongues tie. Once, after a trip with my younger brother to the park, "he" asked my brother what his name was in front of my grandparents. I was given my mother's surname when I was born. Strictly speaking, I was given my grandpa's surname. According to Grandpa, although my father was not a "living-in" son-in-law, which would have diminished his naming rights, the prenuptial agreement was that the first-born, if it was a boy, would be adopted by my mother's elder brother—Grandpa's son. During the Red Terror, Grandpa explained in detail the justifications to me. He thought such an arrangement could draw a clearer line between my father and me. However my younger brother seemed to be compromised. My grandpa said, "One survivor at a time."

Among the three children, my younger brother seemed to be the closest to our father. At first he adopted our father's surname. Later, after our parents' divorce, his surname was changed to our mother's. On that day in the park, reportedly lured by an ice cream, he agreed to revert to our father's surname. However when they returned home, my younger brother decided not to change after all. Our father burst out laughing because he liked my younger brother's cunning. I guess this incident took place after our parents' remarriage. He wouldn't dare such playfulness before they got back together.

Grandpa's son, the person I had to address as "Dad," died of typhoid when he was seventeen, a year before the outbreak of the Anti-Japanese War, or what historians might call the Second Sino-Japanese War. I was directed to call him "Dad" and my biological father "Father." Dad might have died young, but he was revived whenever we kids disappointed our grandparents or whenever life disagreed with them. He was there all year round in a yellowed family portrait, and his name popped out frequently in the remarks of our grandparents, especially Grandma's. He was so much a presence, like the Kitchen God, in our household that Dad was no stranger than Father to me. According to my grandparents, Dad was the most honest and smartest child you could imagine. He never pestered his parents for nice food, sniffing the fragrance of roasted sesame even if what he really wanted was the baked pancake on which it had been sprinkled. At the old-style private school he was the only pupil never beaten by the tutor's ruler. Later at the public primary school he won prizes including a writing brush and an inkstone. Still later he skipped a grade.

The inkstone I used at home was said to be a prize of his. It survived the Anti-Japanese War and the three-year War of Liberation, as well as the family relocation from Ningbo to three successive addresses in Shanghai, only to see its lid broken into two pieces when I accidentally dropped it. Reddening all over, Grandma was ready to hit me. Grandpa intervened in time. "Take it easy, take it easy. He who breaks a lid also dispels bad luck. Scholars grind through their inkstone by long years of study. May our grandson change his fate through study."

He went on to tell a story. Once upon a time there was a seven-year-old child prodigy in Ningbo who rode on his father's shoulders to attend the Imperial Examination at the county level. An amused County Magistrate offered to make him a *xiucai* (one who passed the Imperial Examination at the county level) without sitting the exam if he could match two antithetical couplets perfectly. The County Magistrate said, "Riding the father like a horse." The child prodigy responded, "Hoping the son becomes a dragon." The County Magistrate said, "A young scholar drapes his blue gown onto the floor." The child prodigy answered without thinking, "A senior official points his red hat at the sky." The County Magistrate roared with laughter, and everything was fine.

Everything was fine with me too. After hearing those stories, I was determined to win a prize or skip a grade to make my grandparents happy, but my wishes never came true. Dad was too perfect to exist on earth. God called him back to Heaven to spare him the worldly suffering and the imminent Anti-Japanese War. He caught a cold on a boat trip to sweep our ancestral tombs in Ningbo. It rained heavily. He took off his gown to shelter Grandma, exposing himself to the rain. After his death, guilt drove Grandma, together with my mother, into a church and she almost converted to Christianity.

His condition improved briefly two days before his death. Grandma said she had no idea at that time that it was a momentary recovery just before death (although I found out later that his symptoms hardly qualified as "momentary recovery just before death"). He said he was starving and would like to have some braised pork in brown sauce, having seldom demanded specific foods in his seventeen years of life. Grandma scrambled to make a bowlful of braised pork, which he devoured together with two bowls of rice. That night his fever came back and he passed out. When he came to, he said he heard people walking on the roof and barking military orders. Grandma said he did that to warn the family against the Japanese invasion the following year.

In the family portrait, he wore a long gown with a mandarin jacket and a skullcap. His round face resembled mine in a way, which was weird because we were not related by blood. My mother was not his biological sister. My grandparents found her on a road when she was not yet one month old. I found this out when, at the age of thirteen, I rummaged through a folder where my mother kept blank printing paper and unused account books. Some paper with writing had been inserted there in her absent-mindedness. Only years later did I learn that what I had stumbled onto was the introduction to her divorce petition. There was also a letter in her handwriting, whose first part had gone missing, which read, "My parents have been pressing me to get married. I'm suffering. Please take me away." My intuition came into play at once. I judged this was a call for help to her lover, although the addressed might be a girlfriend of hers. No, it must be a man, a suitor of my mother's. If their scheme had worked, I wouldn't have been born at all. What a close call! I wondered what had prevented this white knight from rescuing my mother from my father, and therefore from giving birth to me. The thought of people having fought over the circumstances leading to my birth sent shivers down my spine.

Why were they so careless? Couldn't they just have kept me in the dark forever now that I had been born? Pain gripped my heart. Other kids spoke of their parents, grandparents, and even great grandparents with deep familiarity, whereas I had to hem and haw when asked. I was like Chenxiang in the legend *Lotus Lantern,* child of a goddess and a mortal, who grew up unaware of his ancestry. How I regretted reaching for the nice paper in my mother's folder! How ignorantly blissful I would have been! I already knew too many things I didn't want to know, and now this. Worse still, what I knew couldn't be unknown. In the days following, I observed my grandparents and my mother closely for anything extraordinary that I had failed to notice before, anything that hinted at their adopted relationship. There was nothing. Mother offered whatever nice food she bought to my grandparents first, as usual. My grandparents saved the best food for us kids, as usual. They scolded my mother and us kids whenever offended, as usual. And smacking befell us kids at their will, as usual. My mother went on being docile and obedient, upholding the family tradition of a date-specific vegetarian diet. She didn't show any sign of discontent. They were just like normal parents and child. I felt relieved.

Years later, Mother had to show me a copy of her second divorce petition, behind the back of my siblings, so that I could state my case clearly to the Red Guard Headquarters and the Municipal Letters and Visits Office for the latter to clarify my class status. As I read the document, out of the corner of my eye I caught her looking at me dejectedly. Then and there her face seemed to wither and yellow, age spots bursting out on her forehead and cheeks all of a sudden. I blinked. The illusion was gone. Mother still looked young, in fact younger than her peers. In the ordinary course of events, I should have stared at her for a few seconds to show how terrified I was at certain contents in the document, but her dejection was too much for me to add another blow. I read on calmly. She must have felt surprised. As I turned over a page, she rose and moved away. A slight sigh escaped her lips, as if she were limp and feeble all over. I could even sense the soreness of her waist. Maybe my calmness boded more ill to her than fuss. Maybe I should have put on some appropriate act. However since nobody had prepared me on how to act out my three-year-long trauma in a few minutes without overstating it or understating it, I didn't try.

Father and Dad went to the same class in the same primary school. I don't remember Father's year of birth or his symbolic animal in the Chinese zodiac, although I was told once. Anyway he appeared to be senior to my mother by more than ten years. His father was a rather famous practitioner of traditional Chinese medicine in Ningbo. However the old man forbade his sons to study medicine, for in his opinion, doctors ruined their chances of a better next life because they might kill patients by mistake. As I saw it, he was either a mediocre doctor or a wrongdoer. At best he suffered from "morality induced neurosis." Not particularly happy with such a grandpa, I've never bothered to look up our family tree at Ningbo's renowned private library, Tianyi Pavilion, which has been in existence since the Ming dynasty.

After the Anti-Japanese War, Father became a traveling trader in Sichuan province. By then his father had died, but the fact that a high-school graduate, quite a rare thing at that time, became a traveling trader convinced me he was not as smart as I was at school. How shameful! He didn't fare well as trader, either. He was robbed of his goods and thrown out. It must have hurt when the bandits didn't invite him, an intellectual in his time, to stay as an advisor. Starving, Father, the outcast, saw a recruitment bulletin for military police in the Nationalist army. If the robbers didn't want him, why not play a cop? An army burning with righteous indignation is bound to win. He got himself recruited.

For a long time I couldn't figure out what the military police was. It was part of armed forces but much more disreputable than the average armed forces. If a person had been conscripted by the Nationalist army, after 1949 he could still be invited to tell his sufferings in the old society and his happiness in the new. On the other hand, I knew it was bad to be a military policeman, even several years before the 1967 issuance of the public notice, *Regulations on Strengthening Public Security Work during the Cultural Revolution*.

When I was in first or second grade, I told my classmates that my father was a Nationalist military policeman. What I meant was he had just been a "man," like an artilleryman, a footman or a tankman, not an officer. To my shock they made a fuss about it. Later my grandparents told me off severely. I was determined to find out what the military police really was, without asking others, only to be more confused than ever. True, the Japanese military police put the resistance fighter, Zhao Yiman, on the torture rack, but the Nationalist military police didn't drive bamboo nails into the fingers of Jiang Zhuyun! I guess what made my father's case worse was instead of being conscripted, he volunteered. When I became a more sophisticated middle school student, I blamed him for being too honest. Couldn't he have just said he was conscripted? Since he clearly admitted that he had volunteered, I had to stick to his version in all my personal statements. Therefore I hated his stupidity as well as his being a reactionary.

Father was said to have worked for two years as a clerk in the military police, never fighting any battles or killing any people, which I reiterated when telling my life story. Even if I condemned him, I didn't want him to be a murderer of innocent people. After this stint in the military police, he happened to arrive in Shanghai, either because of redeployment or a home leave, where he ran into my grandparents. For some reason Grandpa took a liking to him, a fact that Grandma used in order to shut Grandpa up whenever they had a fight, "You told us to trust your judgment, what now? What is he good for? You said he was honest and reliable. He even knew where our ancestral tombs were, very convenient in the future. What now?" Grandpa would shrug her off by assuming a posture of meditation, the eyes contemplating the nose and the nose contemplating the mind. I have never managed to look as inscrutable as he did.

Anyway, at Grandpa's insistence, my father left the military police and married my mother. Come to think of it, once when Grandma repeated her accusation, my mother said pointedly, "You were on his side at that time." Grandma choked and fell silent. Later I read in my mother's divorce petition that she had eventually succumbed because Grandma had knelt down in front of her, crying and threatening her with suicide. It was beyond me why my grandparents' good opinion of my father eventually turned into disdain. He was just a classmate of their diseased son, after all. My grandparents apparently covered all marital costs and my father moved in. Moreover they supported him through a long period of unemployment. Besides, while my father was not strictly speaking a "living-in" son-in-law, he had agreed to let me adopt their son's surname. This hardly seemed to be a fair deal.

Was the idea of taking care of the ancestors, through tomb-sweeping and other rituals, so important that my grandmother would sacrifice her daughter's happiness? I had no clue. Hopefully experts who study my work will dig the truth out.

When I came to cast my eyes around for a life partner, there were two key criteria in addition to the usual considerations even though I couldn't verbalize them very well. First, I would never live with my wife's family, even if her family were way better than mine. Second, I would never marry a girl who had dated the same man for two years previously (later I relaxed it to three years), even if she swore there was no lingering affection any more. Like matter, emotions are indestructible. They get transferred from one object to another, from one form to another. Or they go into dormancy for some time. Never believe that you can snuff out an emotion or wipe from your memory a person you loved or hated. I have witnessed the revival of dormant feelings. For example the baffling wail of a baby waking up from its afternoon nap. My sense of humor goes sour whenever a baby does that. I'm talking about my son. When he cries on other occasions, such as when I have just given him a spanking, the sorrow seems to eat his heart, the childish cuteness of which makes it very hard for me not to smile. However his wail after a noon nap seems to rub the wrong nerve of mine. My chest is so charged that I can almost picture sparks raining down inside it. If I manage to refrain from hitting him, I have to leave immediately.

We human beings are whipped around like spinning tops by emotions all our lives. There is no way to stop. Children wail because they can't help it. Likewise we spin because we can't help it either. Spinning tops differ from one another by the center of gravity. If the center of gravity is well positioned, then the top spins smoothly and steadily. If not, then the top wobbles. The former is good and normal whereas the latter, bad and abnormal. Kids in Shanghai nickname the top a "miserable wretch." How wise the Shanghai residents are!

When I was five, my mother asked for a divorce on the grounds of incompatible "political" divergence. According to my grandparents, there were other reasons. My father was muddle-headed, putting others ahead of his family. Grandpa found him a job as an accountant at a factory owned by his friend. In a few months' time he dipped into the till to help a friend in need. Mother paid the owner back with Grandpa's money, but of course he had to let Father go. Later, at another job, he didn't bring his entire monthly salary home. Upon investigation they found out that he had also kept his bonus to himself. Challenged by Mother, he couldn't explain where the money had gone. However both my grandparents and my mother refused to believe that he could have spent the money on gambling or visiting prostitutes.

I doubted those pretexts for their divorce as soon as I had enough senses. If they had fallen out with each other over such issues, they would have divorced before I was five. How I wished that they had divorced before my birth, but certainly I still had to be born, because otherwise who would the person making the wish be? Moreover it would have belittled my mother to claim that she asked for a divorce on financial grounds. Although she had never been rich, she had never thought highly of money either. Like parents, like daughter. My grandparents had never been stingy. They took the greatest pride in the fact that during the three-year-long Great Chinese Famine, even if they had to sell an entire suite of rosewood furniture, they had never begrudged buying eggs at five jiao each, pork shoulders and ribs, or using pastry coupons. The nutrition of the three kids always came first. Even so, Mother's generosity dwarfed theirs. Grandpa often spoke of our mother in front of her, "You mother doesn't care for money. She says, 'Dad, don't always talk about money.' She doesn't talk about money at all." Grandma kept attributing Father's cunning and greed to Mother's generosity. Mother had even helped Father lie to my grandparents on money issues. So Grandma said that Mother lost her good sense when she tried to be nice to someone. No, they didn't divorce over money issues. They did it for "political" reasons. That was why the court granted the divorce readily.

Some twenty years later, when my mother tried to divorce her second husband, it turned out to be quite a nasty project. It lasted two or three years, with many twists and turns. It was like they were chewing some old bubble gum; although the bubbles became fewer and fewer, they kept chewing it, while we onlookers prayed that they would spit it out, the sooner the better. When it was finally over, Mother had aged so dreadfully that she looked like the peasant girl, Xi'er, from the *White-Haired Girl,* after hiding out in the mountains for years. All because this divorce was apolitical.

A year after their divorce, my parents remarried, for which I bore a grudge against Mother for quite some time. She made an already complicated situation even more complicated. She defeated my efforts to polish her image. After telling my classmates how she had joined the Youth League ahead of most other people, and how she had placed political righteousness above family loyalty, I was worked up into a lather when it came to her marriage. Eloquence, like a biscuit, turns soft with too much saliva. Of course Mother had her justifications. My newborn sister had to be fed and couldn't wear our old clothes. Grandpa's company had recently been nationalized. Since Chairman Mao voluntarily cut his own salary, Grandpa had to follow suit and saw his income shrink by more than thirty yuan.

Also, Father had been begging for a second chance. Mother asked her superiors to make inquiries at the Publication Bureau where Father worked. They found out that Father had not only been forgiven for mistakes made in the past, but also awarded a book for meritorious service to the illiteracy elimination endeavor. The Deputy Bureau Director even wrote Mother a letter to encourage her to get back together with Father, as a way to educate and help a person willing to follow the lead of the Communist Party. The letter made up her mind. However at the time she showed it to me, the Deputy Bureau Director was under investigation as a suspected traitor. I thought it over and decided not to show it to people at the Red Guard Headquarters and the

Municipal Office of Letters and Visits. It wouldn't help my case. Anyway the remarriage was an unnecessary and unwise move without a single redeeming feature.

Nevertheless, Mother's revelation of the divorce petition made me think about the other person responsible for bringing me into this world. My awareness stretched as thin as the soup ladled out to refugees. I had to rack my brain before recalling his taking my younger brother to the park and coming back joking about his surname change. I also recalled that he had once taken me to his workplace. It might have been a neighborhood factory because the staircase leading up to his attic office was very narrow. He left me alone there for hours with a sheet of paper, a pencil and a cigarette packet. He told me to copy the flying horse on the cigarette packet, but my drawing looked like anything but a flying horse. Later he came back and showed me how to draw it in few strokes. In the afternoon he took me to watch a movie. He said it was a wonderful film produced in Hong Kong. I only remember seeing all kinds of women take out their handkerchiefs to cover their noses. I was fascinated, but when Grandma asked me if I had enjoyed the day, it suddenly occurred to me that I shouldn't tell the truth. So I said no, at which she stroked my head.

One event stood out in my memory. It took place when Mr. Cheng, my enemy since our previous lives, was in charge of our class. On a day when an angry Mr. Cheng detained me after school, Father happened to come to pick me up. Thinking Father was the patriarch of our family, Mr. Cheng complained at length to him before letting me go. Father then seized the rare opportunity to wield his authority over me by making a show of kicking me in the ass as we were leaving the school, barking, "F--k, go home this minute!"

Our school was located on the second floor of a building, and a terrazzo staircase about a meter in width led down to the first floor. His kick scared the shit out of me. I guessed I must have committed some mistake so serious that even "he," the person least heard in our family, raised his voice at me.

I mingled immediately into a crowd of students on their way down. He didn't catch up. The idea of running away seized me. I sprinted along the alley, heading for the main road. After making a right turn when I reached it, I made for the right side hall of a temple that housed statues of all kinds of deities, the Hall of the Arhats. It was a frequent haunt for students, whereas the old ladies preferred the opposite side hall where the statue of the Goddess of Mercy was placed. There was a wooden plaque in front of each Arhat, which indicated the birth years and zodiac animals of those under the patronage of the respective "perfected person." It was our favorite pastime to check out our patron Arhat and the associated prospects. It was said that one's fate was correlated to one's patron Arhat. If he looked benevolent, one would be lucky, and if he looked ferocious, one would have bad luck. However there were few Arhats in the hall that looked as handsome as I was. The plaque with my birth year and symbolic animal on it was placed in front of the same Arhat as before, one with hands stretching out of his eyes and eyes protruding from his palms. He certainly was not handsome, but I was not sure whether he was ferocious or not, even though I had compared his looks with all the other Arhats.

After the Hall of the Arhats I looked around the Mahavira Hall and the Hall of the Goddess of Mercy. I didn't dare to kowtow, which would be a serious offense if some classmate reported it to Mr. Cheng. The temple was going to close for the night. I left. It was getting dark. My stomach rumbled much earlier than usual, but I didn't dare to go home. I turned over in my mind the implications of an Arhat with hands in eyes and eyes in hands. I walked toward the alley near the stop of Bus No. 14, where many classmates lived. In my imagination, my exile had already become public knowledge. If I showed up there, some classmate who wanted to become my sworn brother would offer me some money and a grain coupon to buy a baked pancake and a fried dough stick. Strangely, no classmate was hanging out in the alley. The fragrance of soybean oil in the air reminded me that they must be having supper at home. Hunger killed the romance of exile. As I walked from one alley to another my fear intensified. My grandparents must be outraged, and my father must be speaking all kinds of ill about me to make them give up on me. Just then, I heard Grandma call out my name. I answered in a loud voice and dashed toward her, only to find the caller was a strange old lady with a Ningbo accent. Tears welled up. If I went home right now, I could certainly have a good cry when I reached home, and my grandparents might take me in again. The thought drove me home, into the common kitchen, up the stairs, through the inquisitive looks of our neighbors, and there, the door to our room!

Grandpa asked from the darkened front room, "Have you found him?" I hurried to dry my eyes, because I knew tears were not necessary. Grandma, Mother and Father returned one after another. They had each set out in a different direction to look for me, but somehow had all missed me. When Grandma asked me why I had run away, I cast a glance at Father.

Grandma said, "The truth. Never mind him!"

I said, "Father kicked me and used the F-word …"

I had barely finished before she pointed an angry finger at Father. "How dare you treat a child like that! You scared him. He is a timid boy. Why did you kick him with your leather shoe? Did you think you were still a military policeman? If kids are naughty, teach them a lesson at home. Don't do it outside. We just asked you to pick him up this one time and you ruined it! What if he never came back? What if he was kidnapped?"

Father glared at me as if threatening retaliation. I was not afraid at all. From then on an impression was engraved in my mind: He doesn't love us. He is mean to us. He is not a good father.

When I was nine, Mother filed for a second divorce from him. The fault was his again. In the heat of another movement, he suddenly confessed to having concealed firearms for a friend on the eve of Liberation, which he had never mentioned before. Since this was again a political wrongdoing, Mother broke up with him without hesitation. He had violated one of the conditions of their remarriage. Later, when Grandma scolded my younger brother, she said, "Liar, liar. If you go on lying you will suffer, just like your father." Lying was Sin No. 1 in our family. My younger brother was the only one to brave it. My younger sister and I never dared.

It was a summer day. It was my first time seeing adults cry. That was some crying. Mother and Father sat writing at our round dinner table. Wearing a short-sleeved white blouse and a short-sleeved white shirt respectively, they appeared solemnly calm, like two snow mountains facing each other. Tears streamed down their cheeks, turning them almost transparent like window panes washed by a downpour. Despite the torrential tears they didn't howl or sob. If I had cried that much, my throat would have jammed, my scalp would have gone numb and my fingers cramped. Yet they kept talking and writing.

I only remembered him saying, "For the sake of our three kids, please think twice."

"No. No." Mother shook her head violently, spraying tears in arcs. "I have to do this for the kids' sake."

I was fascinated by the way adults cried. So elegant, so serene and so beautiful. It reminded me of thawing rivers in movies. I had a better opinion of Father.

The next day Father moved back to the factory dorm. We kids didn't feel any difference. His presence had never counted. About half a year later, he left Shanghai for a reform-through-labor farm. According to Grandma, he had been so bored at the dorm that he volunteered to go. During the Cultural Revolution, Mother asked her superiors to make inquiries at his work unit. They found out that the verdict handed out to Father during that movement (even today I have no idea which movement) was: "Work under mass supervision. No labeling necessary." Grandma might have been right. However when I retold the event to the Red Guards, none of them believed me. Later I realized that if

I had been a Red Guard, I wouldn't have believed it either. So I stopped explaining.

Grandma also said Father volunteered to go to the farm for an evil reason. He didn't want to pay our child support, which, according to the court ruling, amounted to ten yuan per month per kid until we were old enough to work. He stopped paying when he went to the farm. Later his work unit explained to us that he was no longer able to pay since he no longer collected salary. Even if we took him to court, the court order couldn't be enforced. To make matters worse, Grandpa had just retired at the age of sixty-nine, his pension thirty yuan less than his last salary. In later life Grandma brought up old scores again and again. She blamed Grandpa for bragging to others how he had insisted on retirement despite his leaders' plea for him to stay for two more years. Why did he have to brag? Didn't he know there would be consequences? Smart as Grandpa was, he blundered. Pride and vanity, they are indeed the downfall of man! Subsequently our family went into hardship, as did the entire country. Three years later, the circumstances for the entire country looked up, but our financial situation wouldn't improve until four or five more years down the road.

"Pest! Poison! You will come to no good!" Whenever we were hard up, Grandma would curse Grandpa and then Father, or the other way round. We grew up sucking hatred for him from those curses.

When I was eleven, the pest suddenly wrote to say he would like to see us kids on his business trip to Shanghai. How bold of him to demand a meeting after cutting us off for so long! Flustered, my grandparents and my mother held a lengthy closed-door consultation, after which they broke the news formally to us.

How we wished that he wouldn't come. Meeting a bad guy couldn't be good. We wondered why our grandparents and mother hadn't rejected him outright, if they really hated him so much. Their weak-mindedness put us in an awkward situation. I was determined, however, to give him the cold shoulder. I must place righteousness above family loyalty.

He showed up all of a sudden.

At dusk on that day, my younger brother and I were allowed ten minutes to play outside. His head popped above the top of the stairs just as we reached the door. Having not seen him for two years, I couldn't have conjured up his image with closed eyes. It was a marvel that I recognized him at one glance. He recognized us too and grinned. I was somehow rooted to the spot, forgetting to announce his arrival to my grandparents. He was approaching. I looked up at him slack-jawed—I must have been possessed. His gaze drew hatred and revolutionary determination out of my head like a syringe. Leaning against the door frame, with its flaking paint, wearing a red scarf and a Young Pioneer Branch Leader's badge on my left arm, I grinned back ingratiatingly like a beggar, and my hands twisted, not knowing what to do. I fixed my gaze at his thin lips. The slight curve below his nose was much more handsome than mine. I spoke tentatively, "Father." My younger brother followed suit. His right hand patted me on a shoulder and his left caressed my younger brother's head.

"Haven't forgotten me, have you?" We giggled. It wasn't until Grandma came out that I was jostled into reality. How silly I had been to make a public show of my lack of balls.

He stayed in Shanghai for about a week. During the first two days he slept at a hotel and ate at our place. Later, to save him trouble, we put a square table and a round table together for him to sleep on. I'm not sure if he took us kids out, but I am very sure that even if he did, my mother did not join us. Since I had been weak enough to address him as Father upon our first meeting, I had to carry on. Therefore I prayed for his departure. Finally he left. God must have heard my prayer, because we never saw each other again.

I kept this visit secret from my teachers and classmates. Even if the Red Guards threatened me with metal belt buckles, I insisted that we hadn't met since I was nine. In case someone blew the whistle I was determined to claim that my memory had slipped. Nevertheless it remained a constant worry. How could I not hate him for imposing tragedy after tragedy on me?

A year passed after his visit. One night, I suddenly woke up and found myself lying on my stomach. I usually slept through the night. And I hadn't had a nightmare. I was very alert, although I often fell back into slumber after waking up in the morning. My pillow was wet. I must have dribbled in my sleep. How embarrassing! I turned over, trying to dry it with the warmth of the back of my head. It was then I found, to my surprise, that Grandma was sitting by my bed. She caressed my arm. After a while she said, "He is dead." I was at a loss. Grandma spoke again, "There is a telegraph. He drowned."

Now I realized who she was talking about and that they were tears wetting my pillow. But why did she cry? Grandma's caress was so soothing that I felt as if floating on clouds. "What a hard lot for you all. Ah, things aren't going your way," she mumbled. I didn't get it. Why were things not going our way if our father was dead? It was him alive that had us on tenterhooks. Drowsiness overcame me. I buried my face in the pillow. Grandma immediately flipped me over, scolding, "Don't pick up his habit. He always slept face down, and he ended up drowning in the river." Now the terror really struck home. Something huge had happened. I closed my eyes at once, pretending to sleep. Then I was asleep.

The adults were very tense the next few days fearing that he had committed suicide. Relief came when an official letter from the farm and the coroner's certificate arrived. Both stated that he drowned when bathing in the river. They decided to neither go to his farm nor wear black mourning bands for him. I supported the second part of their decision wholeheartedly. Four years later, I was able to tell the Red Guards righteously, "I didn't even wear a mourning band when he died!" This was the key reason why the Red Guards didn't label me as a "stigmatized son." Consequently I didn't take note of the date he died. For me, he is a shadow without a birthday or a death anniversary. He has attached himself to me. I live, he lives. I die, he die. This is my biological father.

Years later I read a short story in a newspaper in which a veteran cadre persecuted during the Cultural Revolution entrusted her soon-to-be orphan daughter to the care of a ward nurse as she was on her deathbed. When prompted the girl went up to the nurse and called her "Mother." I felt queasy. Afterward, when I met the author I told her that, in my experience, the natural reaction for the girl would be to resist calling anyone else "Mother." I didn't tell her, though, that I had never since addressed anyone else as "Father" or even "So-and-so's Father." "Father" had become a taboo for me. It belonged to one man only. I might be the only contribution this man made to the world. I had to reserve an exclusive title for him. A girlfriend broke up with me because of this peculiarity of mine. When my mother married her second husband, I didn't bend under pressure from the adults. After hours of deadlock we compromised with the term "Dad." To me, "Dad" had been my grandfather's son, whose surname I adopted and whose death occurred before my birth. If the new guy liked sharing the term with a dead man, so be it. I almost snickered when he responded solemnly to it the first time, because I was picturing him in "Dad's" yellowed skullcap.

Despite my hatred for my father and my fear of his impact, his estate was sent home. We were his only heirs. A tattered suitcase, some old clothes. The dome-shaped mosquito net was the most valuable of all, although the bamboo frame was missing.

I can't explain my extraordinary enthusiasm for this mosquito net when getting ready to go to the countryside. I forewent, voluntarily, the square mosquito net that was rationed out to youth dispatched to rural areas, which cost about seven yuan. My frugality seemed unnecessary. Rational as I am, I have a case for almost my all actions, even if extremely foolish. But impulse outweighed reason on this occasion. Taking such a net with me was absolutely irrational, because it associated me immediately with a father whose existence I definitely did not wish others to pry into. Furthermore a dome-shaped mosquito net standing out among the square nets grabbed attention from my new co-workers. They swarmed to size me up. Once they found out that I was not a conqueror but a fool, bullying kicked in. The dome-shaped mosquito net brought suffering to me, but the suffering seemed to be strangely satisfactory. It rubbed my nerves like a sponge on a body; the harder it went, the greater the pleasure. I can't tell whether I chose the net for the sensation or I discovered the sensation because of the net. Anyway I made a burden for my own back, just like my father.

IX

A trolley bus pulled in and then pulled out. I caught a glimpse of a person in black. It vanished through a gray iron gate on the opposite side of the road.

Raven!

An odor of bad eggs surged from my stomach. This must be a telegraph from Destiny.

Raven! I had not seen her since job assignments started, even though I went to school almost every day. Now, on a day when I had neither school nor her on my mind, I ran into her. It must have been predestined. Raven—this was a nickname that my classmate Auntie gave her in the second term of junior high but whose significance I only started to appreciate now. Great. I wouldn't let it go, whether it was predestination or coincidence. Ms. Dong. Dong Yiren. I must track her down and confront her, so that she would never forget me for the rest of her life.

I walked toward the gray iron gate. How long had I been staring at it from across the road? I had no idea. I didn't have a watch. I just felt my body turn hot and cold and then hot again, like a malaria patient. I had wondered why I was rooted to the spot. Now I knew. My feet had hearkened unto Destiny ahead of my brain.

I walked tall and resolute toward the gate. I didn't come to bid a humble farewell to my alma mater—alma mater, was it! No. I came on a mission assigned by Destiny.

I pushed the gate open. The old hunchbacked janitor poked his head out of his prison-cell office. His eyes twinkled. He recognized me. His smile felt like a greasy cloth mopping my heart. I could see me, a black dot, in his turbid pupils. I had always smiled and nodded at him in the past. No, it was not to show respect. He had given me a fright on our first meeting and the impression never improved. I smiled to win his favor so that he wouldn't demand my student ID. My smile must be more disgusting than his. My student ID was in my plastic wallet. I planned to burn it as soon as I got my employee's card in Chongming. How I wish to burn up my petty smile and the place that made me smile so pettily!

The sports field came into view. How time flew! I still remembered the first time I walked through the gate four years ago. No sooner had I entered than I was captivated by the five enormous plane trees on the edge of the sports field. Specks of golden sunlight were dancing on their lush green canopies. The chirping of cicadas in the branches was so boisterous that one almost felt lifted into air. I rushed toward a tree, stretching my arms wide to embrace it. Tree bark rubbed against my white shirt and my chest. I pressed myself against it, reaching out as far as possible. A strange sensation arose as my cheek came into contact with the uneven bark. Unable to see my own fingertips, I pouted like fish.

"You there, how far have I gone?" My companion didn't reply.

I dug my fingernails into the trunk. They started to burn. I backed off to check the two shallow marks I had made. They didn't even make it around half the circumference. I briefly considered trying again, but the stains on my white shirt front boded ill, so instead I went to find my friend. He was drinking at the water fountain. All five shiny copper taps were occupied. Girls wiped the fountain with their handkerchiefs before drinking. When it was my turn, I pushed the button as I leaned close. A spout of water shot toward the roof of my mouth. Part of it got deflected and sprayed out like a mist. The remainder rushed down my throat like water falling into an abyss. A white dragon rose from the abyss to my nasal cavity, where it split into two. One invaded my brain and overturned the ninety-nine urns of vinegar stored there. The other swam out of my nostril to transform into a rainbow. I hurried to straighten up. The water spout from the shiny tap now attacked my chest. My red scarf seemed to drip blood, my white shirt dazzled like melting snow, and my exposed chest seemed as tender as quick-boiled lotus root.

I could hear even myself laugh. Having recently experienced an adolescent change of voice, I croaked like the toy bamboo machine gun with which I used to play.

How did the campus look now? The plane trees were bare. Gruesome wounds where branches had been pruned were still raw. A few fallen leaves lingered around the meager earth at the foot of the trees. Their juice having been sucked out by the north wind, the yellowish leaves were so dry that one blow could reduce them to powder. One leaf looked damp. Maybe someone had pissed on it. Copper colored, it smelled like rusty copper, too. A few grayish sparrows hopped languidly on the grayish cement, hardly flapping their wings. One of them was pecking at the little cones on a broken plane tree twig. The red-and-white net had already vanished from the basketball hoop. The backboard was so weathered that it looked like a grubby sore. I didn't have the heart to approach the water fountain. Having been out of use for over two years, it must look pathetic. The water marks on the light ochre terrazzo fountain would have dried into rings of wavy powder that one could wipe off with one's fingers. They were the wreckage of water, zombies of the living, and mummies from ages long gone. They were cruel reminders of once vivacious beings. They forced you to recognize that part of your life, your prime, your youth, had faded away, and that all your efforts to keep their appearance made you all the uglier.

This was my alma mater! Grandpa had once told me that the Bodhisattva would enlighten a mortal by making him wake up to find the young woman sharing his bed first turned into a wizened old lady and then a skeleton. Who was trying to enlighten me by luring me to this sight of ruin? What was I supposed to comprehend? In fact, why bother bringing me here? I had no attachment to it whatsoever. My alma mater, what had it given me? Idols fallen from the altar, a kick on my bottom, and a bruise that never went away. There had never been any genuine spring. Instead its moldy air had spoiled my innocence. There had never been any real garden. Instead the ferocious weeds almost smothered my conscience. Had it taught me the true, the good and the beautiful? No. What was true was the law of the jungle, what was good was playing the perfect courtier, and what was beautiful was a forced smile.

The usual associations with schools—knowledge, friendship, teachers as loving gardeners, students as bees busy gathering honey, warm sunshine, gentle breeze and fine drizzle—were all just spit flying from the mouth of a jester. Worse, they were tricks that made you a lamb to the slaughter. I might one day return again to my alma mater. But by then I must not feel useless and helpless. Instead I must have made a name for myself. I would not return to honor the place, but to show it that a life it had tried to trample on had rebounded, the moldy taste driven out of its marrow cavity, blood flowing red and strong, wounds healed, and skin glowing.

I daydreamed in the company of cowering sparrows. Images swarmed inside my head. Like the poor Little Match Girl in the fairy tale, I was carried away by illusion. There and then, I forgot my mission. I became a defeated general who, facing the battleground strewn with bodies and nursing his wounds, swore that he would make a comeback.

It had been a typical downcast winter afternoon, three days before my departure to Chongming. Heavy clouds draped the sky. Occasional rays poked through them here and there. The northwest wind felt as mild as scratches from kitten paws. That was why I could daydream. If the wind had been stronger, my brain wouldn't have stored up enough energy to daydream. And so, whenever I felt like daydreaming in the wintry fields of the farm, I put on a thickly-padded cotton hat with fluffy flaps.

The next day I got the passage ticket to Chongming. It read: Steamer departs from Dada Terminal at 6:30 a.m.

"Where is Dada Terminal?" I asked Hong Liu.

"The same as Shiliupu Terminal," he answered.

"How come Shiliupu Terminal has been renamed Dada Terminal?"

"Maybe its real name is Dada Terminal, and Shiliupu is its alias," he said. "Like a person, it can have several names." Apparently uninterested (I was going to find out very soon what was on his mind), he said he would come to pick me up at 5:30 so as not to miss the ship. Seeing my frown he said, "It's no big deal even if we miss the ship. We could stay at home a few more days and buy another ticket on our own."

My nervousness grew but I didn't want to make it obvious. My manner should be as free and easy as his. Yet words failed me.

He cackled like a mother hen. "Don't you worry. I'm the team leader. How could I make my team members miss the boat? Zhuge Liang was cautious all his life. So am I."

I was secretly annoyed. If he considered himself a renowned leader like Zhuge Liang, who was I supposed to be? After going home, I asked around. No one seemed to know of Dada Terminal. Everyone said the steamers to Chongming left from Shiliupu Terminal. Worried, I decided to check out Shiliupu Terminal when I got up the next morning. Although it was a landmark in Shanghai, I had never been there. Since I was leaving Shanghai shortly, a stroll there in the daytime wouldn't be an entire waste of time. I hoped secretly to find out that Dada Terminal was actually located in Tilanqiao or Yangshupu, because I would then be able to teach Hong Liu a lesson about arrogance.

To my regret, although Dada Terminal was not the same as Shiliupu Terminal, they were next-door neighbors. To my greater regret, the business district around Shiliupu was substandard. Accustomed to the posher Nanjing Road area, I eyed the few somewhat decent shops with disdain. However, with the clock ticking away, I must make my trip worthwhile. I decided to walk back along the Huangpu River and have another look at the towering buildings on its bank.

Shortly afterward, the familiar ash black campus wall came into sight. I stood, rooted, across from it, until the woman in black lured me into this tomb of a place.

The cold finally roused me. I was alone in this immense enclosure. Not a soul stirred. My voice would echo when I confronted Dong Yiren later. I should plan my exit in case they tried to block me. This idea conjured up a mental picture of Pale Face and his colleagues rushing down the stairs or popping up from underground to besiege me. Heat went up my spine. I saw myself give the hunchbacked old man a punch, flee through the gate, and get on a trolley that was pulling out. There was a dull pain in my wrist. I must have hit the hunchback. I flexed my wrist and stopped daydreaming.

Where was Dong Yiren? These days, teachers were elusive. They didn't have permanent offices or desks. She might be at the former Dean's Office and current Office of the Workers' Propaganda Team. Going there would be putting my own neck into the noose. The only thing feasible was to wait for her here. But how long should I wait? Half an hour? An hour? Since I didn't have a watch, I went to check the electric clock in the janitor's room. The hands stuck at three to nine. I had to resort to the old-fashioned way. There were 60 seconds to a minute and 3,600 seconds to an hour. I would count until 2,000. Where should I stand? Certainly not here in the middle of the road. I went up the steps leading to the West Building, pretending to look at a dilapidated bulletin for execution by firing squad. Two thousand seconds. If Destiny really wanted me to punish this evil woman, she would materialize before I reached 2,000.

She showed up.

My heart skipped a beat when a figure in black turned the corner. I moved toward her. A flame rose from my feet, crawled along my sciatic nerve, hovered around my anus, changed direction and went up from my navel to my chest, where it fluttered like bird wings. She saw me. There was a hint of surprise on her face. My solemn look must have given her a fright, which was exactly what I wanted. From this day on she wouldn't close her eyes without seeing my face! I considered my opening remarks. How should I address her? Her first name, instead of the respectful "Ms. Dong," so that her blood pressure would shoot up at once? Or "Director Dong," with sarcasm? She paused. She was scared. Well done. I must carry on. I must not waste this opportunity for revenge bestowed by the fates.

"Why are you here?" she spoke first.

Great. There was no need to address her. "Do you know I'm going to Chongming?"

"Oh, yeah!" This exclamation reminded me of her overseas background. "You are. When do you leave?"

"Why did you assign me to Chongming?"

"Well," she uttered, "I'm not sure. I've been ill. The Workers' Propaganda Team made the decision."

"How did you grade me?"

"It has slipped my mind. Truly. High blood pressure makes me dizzy and forgetful. I gave faithful accounts of every student to the Workers' Propaganda Team. They told me how they were going to grade students, but I can't remember. I have been dizzy all the time."

She was more tactful than I had imagined, passing the buck without batting an eyelid. The job assignment had been unfair not only in outcome but also in process. They didn't announce the number of jobs available in factories, in rural Shanghai and in rural China. Neither did they reveal how they graded you. They simply mailed a notice to your home. You waited in hope, only to find what was done couldn't be undone. Such calculation was highly unlikely for Lao Lü, the head of the Workers' Propaganda Team. Dull as I was, I could sense her behind the scenes. Her dizziness cost us our youth!

How I wanted to curse her in the most vicious way possible! But I remained speechless. Cheng Yaojin, a Tang dynasty warrior popular in stories, often lost the battle if he failed to kill his opponent with three blows of his axe. Was I as clumsy as he was? My palms sweated. My vocal cords slackened like a broken bicycle chain. I glared, hoping to ignite my anger by looking at her evil, hypocritical face. Then I noticed her weird, beak-like nose. It was several shades yellower than the rest of her face, as if her maker had run short of clay during its creation, therefore having to nip some from elsewhere for her nose. The nose expanded under my glare to take up most of her face. What with her protruding blood-shot eyes and pointed vermillion mouth, she indeed looked like a bird, a raven. Ravens were scavengers, ominous. Maybe I could sneer like the revolutionary hero Yang Zirong, when he faced "Vulture," the bandit head. If I was incapable of cursing, I could at least sneer. If I sneered once, curses would follow.

Sneer, sneer! Pull my mouth sideways, drop my jaw, and utter something. It should be easy …

The sallow, beak-like nose fascinated me. The blackheads were as distinctive as bacteria under a microscope. I had never observed her so closely. I changed my mind. This was too solemn an occasion for sneers. Sneers would make me just a weirdo in her eyes, and she wouldn't feel sorry for what she had done to me. No. I must put an albatross around her neck.

"When are you leaving?" she spoke again. "Have you packed?"

"Yes. My luggage is already on the way."

"That's quick. Fortunately Chongming is not very far away. Come back often to see us."

"Okay."

"Is there anything else I can do for you?"

"No."

"How is your mother? And your grandparents?"

"They're fine."

"You were a good student. You'll have bright prospects in the countryside. I look forward to hearing about your achievements."

I stood by, mute.

"Is that all? If you will excuse me, I have to go to the hospital for my blood pressure. Goodbye!"

She left. What had happened to me? I hadn't come here to hear these remarks.

I could have caught up with her, confronted her, and raised her blood pressure even further, but I didn't, because courage had deserted me.

For the first time in my life I realized what a coward I was.

I was born weak.

Two years after my encounter with Raven, I tried once again to overcome my weakness. I hopped on a trolley bus, determined to steal a ride. In order to facilitate the deed, I had picked a very crowded bus, got on from the door in the middle, and complained loudly, "What a crowded bus! Make room!" Nobody challenged me. Neither of the two conductors stationed at the front and back doors bothered even to bark, "New passengers, ticket please!" The only challenge came from inside me. My back itched, my forehead perspired, butterflies fluttered in my stomach, and my mouth tasted bitter. I started to see my own folly. Why did I put myself in this position? Was it to exercise my guts? What was the use of such guts? Did I plan to break the law or become a spy? What had seized me? I tried very hard to think back, but I seemed to suffer from amnesia. Except for the idea of stealing a ride, everything else in the past had turned into a blur.

Then I recalled an incident when I was just a fifth grader. My classmate and I went into a grocery store to gawk at the sweets and cookies in glass jars. We were standing between a red icebox and a counter displaying bottles of orangeade and milk. A fat woman approached the milk counter with a two jiao bill in her hand. Seeing the sales assistant had turned his back to take some cold drinks out of the ice box for waiting customers, she took a bottle of milk, removed the lid and sipped leisurely. She drank elegantly with her pinky up, the bill between her index finger and middle finger. We were impressed. How clever it was to drink without scrambling for the sales assistant's attention. She finished the milk, replaced the bottle and walked away. We thought she was going to pay but she left the store to join the traffic outside. Stunned by such bold shoplifting, it didn't occur to us to inform the sales assistant until after a minute later. When he understood what had happened, the sales assistant went out to check. The fat woman was nowhere to be seen.

Probably she had influenced me subconsciously, so much so that I decided to defy the norm too. Yes, I had always admired her well-conceived plan and easy manner. However she seemed to have neglected the two onlookers. If the onlookers had been more sophisticated, she might have been caught red-handed. It would be a stain on one's character whether one stole a bottle of milk or a car. The thought of silent onlookers now made my neck stiff. Dark skinned, patches all over my clothes, I didn't look like someone working in a Shanghai factory and carrying a monthly pass. I must be marked. Maybe a ticket inspector would get on the bus at the next stop to check my ticket. Maybe when I got off, a hand would be placed on my shoulder. I would turn back to see a man with a wrinkled face and a grizzled beard who said, "We can't lose our sense of dignity even if we are poor. Don't disgrace the poor!"

Danger was looming ahead, and poetry rushed through my brain. "Dark clouds bearing down on the city threaten to overwhelm it." I must fish or cut bait. "The sea of bitterness is boundless, repent and the shore is at hand." And Chairman Mao wrote, "Heaven would grow old if it had passion. The ruler of the world is time." He instructed us that "we should try our best to minimize unnecessary sacrifice." The trolley bus was literally crawling. We hadn't covered a block yet. A hare and a tortoise agreed to a race. The tortoise fell asleep while the hare kept running. No, the hare fell asleep. No, neither fell asleep. The tortoise climbed onto the head of the hare. It stretched out its neck to touch the finishing line. It won, thanks to its long neck. My fable sounded much more interesting than Aesop's. How could I risk such a good brain? Surely I didn't want to have to lower my noble, wise head to a ticket inspector with a sinister smile, with all eyes were fixed on me in the broad daylight. Why bother? So that I could brag to my co-workers on the farm, my old classmates, my future wife and kids that I had once stolen a ride? With the trolley bus trudging toward the next stop, I still had time to cleanse myself of stupidity. One was no longer stupid if he realized his stupidity. "When one has learnt wisdom in the morning, one may be content to die in the evening." "I reflect on myself three times a day." Did it count as giving in? No, this was the pursuit of truth, the distillation of soul.

"A ticket for 0.4 jiao!"

"Will you please pass it to him? Thanks!"

I felt cool and contented, like a man dunking his head into a spring after trekking in the desert for three days. What a relief! I knew I would come to little in my life. Chickened out of a free ride? Forget it, man. Count it lucky if you had rice and braised pork for every meal!

Back to what happened after my encounter with Dong Yiren. No sooner had I left the school than I ran into Old Lady, Girl, Auntie and Ah-Ming, who cried out at the sight of me. It turned out that they had visited my home to invite me to take pictures with them, but I wasn't there. Old Lady had a camera and some film. He also promised to develop pictures for us for free. He was being generous because he had gotten a decent job at a factory, and his mother allowed him to keep all his wages. All four of them were glad to see me. With Old Lady staying in Shanghai, me going to Chongming, and the two others earmarked for rural China, God knew when we would see each other again. Having never traveled out of Shanghai, I found the provinces Jiangxi and Anhui remote enough, even though they were among the closest to Shanghai, let alone Yunnan province in the far southwest, or Heilongjiang province, way up north.

Even those who had traveled outside Shanghai to exchange revolutionary ideas during earlier days of the Cultural Revolution felt sorrowful at this stage, fearing every get-together to be the last. They cared for me enough to invite me to take pictures with them. I was touched. We walked back to the school. Old Lady led us toward the iron gate.

My heart gave a lurch. "Are we going in?"

"Yes. Let's go to the garden in front of the East Building," Old Lady replied. "The scenery there is pretty good. We could stand by the banister of the stone steps …"

"No," I said, "I don't want to go in. I don't like the school at all."

Old Lady was embarrassed. Of course, having a factory job immunized him to feelings such as mine. Auntie echoed, "Right. Let's not take pictures in there. I would hate to be in there again." Ah-Ming had no preferences. Girl gave it some thought before stating, "Right. Not here." Apparently discouraged, Old Lady managed a smile of tolerance.

It then dawned on me that they wouldn't have bumped into me if they hadn't agreed to take pictures at the school. I ruined their plan. I was quite pleased with myself. I had said what was on the mind of Auntie, Girl and Ah-Ming. People had rallied around me. I was not a good-for-nothing after all. That being the case, I considered myself the director of the photo session. Although I had never used a camera, I gave Old Lady a lot of advice on view finding. In addition I took two pictures of the others, after he had adjusted the shutter speed, aperture and distance. The prints turned out to be as blurry as what an audience would see in a 3D movie if they weren't wearing special glasses. According to Old Lady, I had pressed the shutter too hard and my hand had been shaking at an unusual interval of one-hundredth of a second.

The photo session was so hilarious that I didn't return home until 5:30 p.m. Grandpa's long fingernails were a millimeter away from the tip of my nose. "Where have you been? Things aren't going your way! I told you not to fool around—Hong Liu left just now. He is not going to Chongming and his luggage is back. What will you do now?"

I couldn't react. My emotions had run dry after what had happened that afternoon.

X

A magnitude 6.2 earthquake hit the southern Yellow Sea at 11:38 p.m. on May 21, 1984. Tremors were felt in Shanghai.

The first tremor shook me awake. At first I thought a large truck passing had caused the clattering of window panes and bowls. This happened quite often, it was just that this truck felt like a tank. I had only seen tanks in movies, though. Another tremor hit when I was just about to doubt the appropriateness of my comparison; one should compare unfamiliar things with familiar things, not the other way round. My bed felt like a zigzagging car controlled by a drunk driver. I knew what it was at once: horizontal seismic vibration, something we learned profoundly after the 1976 Great Tangshan Earthquake (in Hebei province) had claimed hundreds of thousands of lives. Such vibrations felt much better than the jolts a boat gave you in a rough sea. Your insides seemed to loosen up like dandelion seeds being blown away.

I didn't move, reckoning it was already too late and, in case of the house collapsing, not necessarily safer to take shelter under the bed. I didn't believe the house would collapse at all. Neither could I picture my being crushed to an instant death. I savored the vibration the way people enjoyed a serenade, so gentle and so tender. It was almost like I was lying on a huge electric massage bed in the moonlight surrounded by glowworms. Can death be this poetic? I didn't think so.

The rocking went on. We should redesign cradles to make

them rock horizontally too. Babies would certainly have sweeter slumber. More rocking. My bare arm felt chilly on top of my quilt. Was God serious this time? Did he really want to take my life? The vibrations stopped as abruptly as they had started. I cast a sidelong glance at my wife, who was asleep with her back toward me, her silky black ponytail spread loosely on the pillow to reveal an elegant neck dyed lilac by the moonlight. It occurred to me that I should wake her up and let her make her own choice in the face of this disaster none of us had foreseen coming, otherwise her ghost might blame me for her death. When I finally made her face me, she was all jitters before opening her eyes.

"Has the alarm clock gone off?"

I was almost amused. About two months before, she made it to her office with only half a minute to spare because the alarm didn't wake us (or probably it didn't go off). Once bitten, twice shy—how true! When she was convinced of the earthquake, she calmed down.

"Might it be something else?"

"No."

"I didn't feel a thing."

"I did. It woke me up."

"Was it bad?"

"Not quite."

"Will there be another quake?"

"No idea."

"What shall we do?"

"Not much we can do. I don't want to leave the house. If it collapses, all the houses in the neighborhood will go down. We might stay alive lying in bed but get crushed outside. It could be a good thing for the three of us to sleep together and die together."

"Okay," she answered without any hesitation, rewarding me for my steadfast love with a kiss on the left cheek.

Then I decided to also give Mother, who was sleeping in the back room, a choice. I called out to her. She turned on a lamp.

After hearing me out, she agreed to my decision immediately and switched off her lamp. She was as indifferent to death as we were.

So, all four of us lay waiting. Our son was still asleep. Aged a year and a half, he was too young to make a choice. If he had been older, I was sure he would have agreed with me too.

Other people stirred. Somebody shouted, "Earthquake, earthquake." The voice pierced the silky night like a spear. My wife nudged me and I stroked the back of her hand. Sometimes we say it best when we say nothing at all. Some neighbors in our building went downstairs and closed the building gate behind them with a slight thud. They moved gingerly, probably not wishing to be known. Nobody panicked, fussed or made a show of evacuation. I congratulated myself on having made the wise decision to spare us being humiliated in front of our neighbors the next day. By half past twelve, seeing no signs of another shock, my wife decided she had had enough. She fell asleep in my arms in no time. If the sky fell and the earth cracked then and there, our bodies would remain so until rescue workers found us. Our serene coziness would certainly take their breath away, although in fact we were seldom that intimate in bed. If that happened, another untruth would be created. I thought to myself, my eyes wide open. I was not afraid. I just wanted to hear more chaos outside. But I was let down. The sound and fury, if there was any, was only one-thousandth of that when the men's national soccer team beat Saudi Arabia four to two, or when the women's volleyball team won a world championship. People's equanimity in the face of death deflated my ego—I had thought I was among the few who were capable of philosophical thinking.

By half past one, there were sounds of doors opening and footsteps on the stairs. Our neighbors returned. The show had come to an end. I went back to sleep, not without regret.

The heated discussion the next day came as a shock. It turned out that sensational things had happened in other parts of the city. The People's Square was packed with folks seeking refuge. Some guy in Jiangwan jumped out of a second-floor window and broke a leg. When residents in an alley in Nanshi swarmed out of their houses, they found a crack in the middle of an asphalt road. Believing it to be a rift, interested onlookers stood on its verge debating and probing until daybreak. A shaken husband jammed all the bank books and the cash from the drawer into the pocket of his pajamas. His wife saw this and got into a physical fight with him. There was no one to stop them, because the neighborhood director for security and safety had taken her family to a safer place. A young mother recovering from hepatitis went immediately to check on her three-year-old son, who was living with her mother-in-law. Although the buses had stopped operating, they were as thronged with people as in rush hour, because according to foreign media, buses had special anti-shock features. The woman walked over an hour to reach her mother-in-law's, only to find that her mother-in-law had left with her son, heading to her house. A smart husband placed a bench at both the head and foot of the bed on which he, his wife and their children huddled, so that falling beams would hit the benches first. Such anecdotes circulated for three days. The more I heard, the prouder I was of myself. I seized every opportunity to mention that I had hardly stirred from bed. Almost always, someone would echo this by saying he or she had simply lain awake, and another person would make a claim of having slept through the night.

People's supernormal detachment in the face of supernormal blows by fate explains a childish question I had when I was young: What about the people who were ordered by Japanese invaders to dig a grave for themselves before being buried alive? Such a death must be far more excruciating than being shot. Why didn't they hit the Japanese with their shovels? Medically speaking, a surge of adrenaline would make a man in crisis incredibly strong. This was how Cai Yongxiang managed to push a log off the railway tracks, single-handedly saving a train full of Red Guards. It was a feat impossible in normal circumstances. Isn't death the ultimate crisis for mortals? Why didn't these people make good use of the adrenaline? What was the point of leaving the adrenaline to the soul (if soul was indeed detachable from the body)?

The answer came to me later. No, I didn't get to it by reasoning. I'd rather use the term "epiphany." It was a sudden realization how childish I had been to raise such a question. A mature person is above it. A mature person accepts destiny and death like the majority of people in history. I couldn't explain when and how the epiphany was attained. The maturity of a person takes place without one being aware of it, just like falling asleep. Anyway, my epiphany about acceptance must have taken place before Hong Liu's sudden exemption from the job assignment to Chongming. I'm as sure of this as I am sure that I fell asleep before 2 a.m. the other day, because I heard our neighbor's Triple Five Brand table clock strike one but not two. That I helped myself to two bowls of rice after hearing about Hong Liu was proof of my epiphany.

On my way to Hong Liu's place, I planned to attack him for keeping me in the dark the day before, when I had asked him about our steamer tickets. However when we met I didn't even mention it. The die had been cast. Scathing remarks were to no avail. Hong Liu apologized profusely. He said the Workers' Propaganda Team had changed their mind at the last minute so that he could help them wrap up job assignments. He was reluctant, but he had to give face to Madam Ma from the Workers' Propaganda Team, showing respect since she had always been nice to him. He would come to the farm where all his best classmates, Zheng Guomei in particular, were assigned, but on a later date. He also said he had sorted things out for me. In fact he would take me to Jing's house this moment, because the latter was totally dependable. Still, I wasn't assured. Several months later, Hong Liu admitted to having told another lie, because Madam Ma was trying to get him reassigned to a factory. Neither Jing nor Commander Hot Water, who was going out with him at that time, was in the know, although they had somehow guessed the truth. I was kept completely in the dark, and I had facilitated it myself. Anyway, one thought persisted in my mind that night: A good horse never grazes on the same pasture twice. Similarly, on the night of earthquake, I tried very hard not to become a laughingstock.

Jing lived in a block of apartments on Fengyang Road, diagonally across from Tongji Hospital. The drab cement walls and staircases gave the impression of a warehouse. A homemade screen partitioned Jing's place of about eighteen square meters into two. The anteroom, which took up about four to five square meters, contained an old-fashioned small square table, a kitchen cabinet and four square stools with chipping paint. All the furniture was well scrubbed. There were several picture frames on a wall. A yellowed family portrait was placed in the center, surrounded by photos of all sizes and ages, including individual photos, group photos, ID photos, artsy photos and landscape photos. There were also some certificates of merit, one was which was awarded to Jing himself, noting that Wang Mingquan was a sixth grader good in study, work and physical training. I immediately felt closer to him. Hong Liu later told me that Jing had made the screen, the tenon joints of which connected in such a seamless way that even a professional carpenter would be impressed. The remaining space behind the screen had to accommodate Jing's mother, his sister, two brothers and Jing himself. After 9 p.m., when they were sure no visitor would intrude, they folded the screen back and set up beds all over the room. The idea of a screen was in itself ingenious.

Jing was not in. Otherwise I wouldn't have had the leisure to size up his home. His older sister emerged from behind the screen to serve us each a glass of sugared water. She struck up a conversation with us before going back behind the screen to mind her own business, at our insistence. Hong Liu and I sat facing each other. He seemed to be a familiar presence here, so much so that the hostess delegated entertaining the guest to him. He fidgeted when Jing hadn't arrived home by 9 p.m. That was when he told me about the screen. The guilt of overstaying our welcome was dwarfed by my anxiety to meet my future protector before leaving Shanghai in two days' time. I could size him up by looking at his photos, as people did before a blind date. I could also ask around. In any case I was going to be with him even if we didn't hit it off. However I just wanted to meet him in person. There was also an element of subtlety in people management. They should realize that I took the initiative in deciding my future instead of depending on others. So I had to stick it out despite the 9 p.m. rule.

At a quarter after nine, Jing came back. Hong Liu swallowed his proposal to leave and raged at him instead for keeping us waiting. Jing smiled nonchalantly, "Funny. We didn't agree to meet at my house."

"We did. I told you I would come. I remember it clearly."

"So do I. You never told me you would come."

"Don't you try to talk your way out of it." Hong Liu turned red to the tips of his ears. "I did so tell you. You must be distracted."

"Well, well, well. Who is trying to talk his way out of it? Who has a better memory, you or me?"

"It has nothing to do with better memory. You're changing the subject."

"Stop accusing me." Jing cast me a glance. "Fine. You told me, and I was distracted. What difference does it make?"

Hong Liu shook his head vehemently to show his distress at someone refusing to acknowledge wrongdoing. Jing asked, "Is this the good friend you talked about?" He stretched a hand to me. Caught by surprise, I hastened to withdraw my hand from my trouser pocket. To my embarrassment, I tore the pocket.

Hong Liu's mood improved. He made formal introductions for us. My first impression of Jing was positive. His features were regular enough but for the slightly slanted eyebrows. When he smiled, his eyes turned into two benevolent slits. Later he told me his mother would slap him if he chewed loudly, even if they weren't urbanites, originally coming from the north of Jiangsu province. Admittedly he managed to speak without a trace of northern Jiangsu accent, so one wouldn't normally suspect his origin. Thinking back, I found his oval face quite typical of Yangzhou natives, but back then Shanghai residents had not developed a sophisticated enough system to tell people from northern Jiangsu apart. His habit of pouting before speaking won the hearts of others easily.

Our three-party talk went on in a cordial and friendly atmosphere but for a slight divergence of opinions toward the end. Hong Liu wanted Jing to fetch me at 5:30 a.m. on the day of our departure, but Jing wanted us to meet at the waiting room or on the boat, because it was very inconvenient to make a detour to my house with his carry-on luggage. Hong Liu spoke against his laziness, but Jing, while smiling, didn't yield. Since silence would be wrong on my part, I told them I knew where Dada Terminal was and could go there on my own. Jing said he knew little about the terminal, so I gave him a briefing. Everybody was happy.

On our way home, Hong Liu talked some more about Jing, how he treated people and good friends in particular with sincerity, how he sometimes acted in a slick but harmless way, and so on. I was grateful but had my own thoughts. I had the vague feeling that Hong Liu wanted to impress me with the power he wielded over Jing, in order to ease my mind. But Jing didn't take orders from him submissively, even if he appeared to be quite agreeable. I decided not to strut in front of Jing in borrowed feathers, but to seek his approval.

When I reached home it was half past ten, very late by the standard then. Grandpa was waiting for me, sitting up in his bed. After telling him about our visit to Jing's house, I said I hadn't changed my mind. His sneer made my hair stand on end. I asked him what was wrong but he waved me to bed, saying, "Leave everything until tomorrow."

I went to bed. Grandpa was still sitting. I shut my eyes, not daring to move a muscle. After a while I was sound asleep.

The next morning, I remembered my promise to meet Ah-

Ming and the others at the People's Park to finish off the film. I wondered if I would be allowed out but I had to try. Indeed Grandpa scolded me. Nevertheless he let me go in the end, telling me to return home as soon as possible and get myself together. I did get myself together, so much so that I didn't enjoy myself at all. By 10 a.m. I returned home.

To my surprise, Grandpa was in the front room looking more refreshed than ever. Without warning he said to me, "You go ahead to Chongming. Don't worry. Everything will be fine!"

I regarded him in stupor, not understanding why there was such a turnaround in his attitude. "I've been to Hong Liu's place," he said, in high spirits, his goatee puffing out like the mane of a galloping horse. "I ran into the guy you call 'Uncle' in Building No. 4. We talked. He called me 'Old Uncle'! No worries. Weren't Hong Liu and Jing both his disciples? He now knows you are my grandson, and he'll treat you with respect. He's just a minor rogue, no big deal. I've seen him and sized him up. Nothing to worry about. Go to Chongming with them."

Only then did I notice that Grandpa's energized look came from his unusual outfit. He was dressed in a brown tweed, Chinese-style lined jacket with cloth buttons on the front, a pair of almost new, dark black twilled satin trousers whose legs were fastened with pale lilac satin ribbons, pale gray Chinese-style yarn stockings, and a pair of black cloth shoes with white soles. Reeking of mothballs, he was no longer his old self, who always wore a loosely-fit, greasy, indigo silk jacket; a pair of loose and worn cotton-padded trousers; and grayish cotton-padded shoes with backs turned in. His almost valiant appearance, now at age seventy-eight, made it easier to believe that he had been a brave man half a century ago.

However his optimism didn't infect me. How could a wizened old man like him inspire awe in a thug, if Uncle in Building No. 4 was indeed a thug? I knew for sure that Grandpa didn't know how to hit deadly acupuncture points in his opponent's body. Neither did he have a large number of followers at his beck and call, like the few surviving ringleaders. Even if he had been part of the underworld, his fellow gangsters would have been dead now. He had never named any friend who, in his seventies or eighties, was still walking the earth. I guessed he must have tried to intimidate Uncle with some old gangster jargon he had learned when he was a traveling trader, and that Uncle played along for the sake of his senility. All kinds of sentiments were flitting around my head as I thought of the disgrace my antique grandpa had brought on me.

Grandpa looked more serious. "You must bear in mind what I'm going to tell you. If you don't, Grandpa can't pick up after you all your life. Don't be intimidated by thugs. They are the shoddy kind of human beings who are the easiest to deal with. Remember these two pieces of advice. First, smart people don't have it all. Thick people have about equal chances. If you are born thick, stay thick, and the worst won't befall you. Don't ever try to look smart. If you do, you will end up neither here nor there. Second, dignity comes from independence. Don't always rely on your friends. China advocates equality and mutual benefits in relationships with big and small countries alike. So should we in interpersonal relationships. 'A hedge between keeps friendship green.' Don't you ever forget!"

XI

It was time to leave.

I thought of looking back as I reached the glass partition door in our room. From now on I would no longer be an official member of this household, although I could visit from time to time. Chances of a permanent reinstatement were slim. The Chairman's instruction to us, to plan for the worst and try for the best, would become my motto. My worst would be farming the rest of my life on the third largest island of our motherland, and my best, coming home, the best place in the world. A final look at my home should give me the drive. It was a little difficult to look back, though. I had slung two carry-on bags onto my right shoulder, one draping over the front and the other on my back. The thin cord tying them together was cutting into the flesh around my neck. One bag contained a change of clothes, toothbrush, toothpaste, enamel mug, towels and so on. The other accommodated a bottle of fried pork shreds with preserved vegetables, a bottle of Chuanxiang Brand chili sauce, some bread, a bar of soap, some toilet paper and several books. All were necessities because we heard that our checked luggage, with the exception of bedding, would arrive much later at the farm than we would, sometimes a week later.

I had planned not to bring any food, bracing myself for the worst possible food in Chongming, because going there should be a clean break from my family and my old self. Then I had second thoughts. The strangers on the farm might not have such a high ideological and political consciousness. What if they offered me food, and I had nothing to offer in return? If I declined, I would alienate myself. If I ate their food for free, I would be seen as a sponger. Therefore I had to bring some food for the sake of civilities, but instead of snacks or fruit (the bread was to be my lunch on the boat), I would bring some well-chosen dishes. Grandma was famous for her fried pork shreds with preserved vegetables, the recipe for which she had inherited from her Ningbo ancestors. As for the chili sauce, I came to know it because some Shanghai students used it to spice up whatever inedible food they encountered on their cross-country trips to exchange revolutionary ideas. They praised it as the best value-for-money condiment. Lu Xun seemed to hold the same view, because he had written that as a southerner in Beijing, he dressed the unfamiliar food with chili sauce.

If chili sauce was a good idea in general, the next step was to find out the best chili sauce on the market. I was told that the most authentic Chuanxiang Brand chili sauce was only available at a store selling delicacies from southern China, located near the Municipal Workers' Cultural Hall. When I saw the long queue outside that store, I was totally convinced. Subsequently I ran home, grabbed an empty bottle, and rushed back to join the queue, wheezing. Once there, I asked regular shoppers in the queue which type of chili sauce offered the best value for money. They each aired their view and we had a very animated seminar on the various values of different Chuanxiang Brand chili sauces. Forty five minutes crept by. In the end I bought broad-bean chili sauce, the cheapest in the store. A small spoon of it sent a burning sensation from my mouth down to my navel. Good. It would serve them right, those co-workers on the farm who had their eyes on my food!

As I just wrote, it was a bit difficult to look back with the two cumbersome carry-on bags. I would have to turn around. However if I did so, my bags would come into contact with a thin board against which my mother's bed and an ancient makeshift wardrobe leaned. Two sheets of pale green PVC, hanging from the ceiling to the floor on opposite sides, gave my mother some privacy. When I was little, I used to act out scenes from *Monkey King*, *Prince Nezha's Triumphs over Dragon King,* and *Wu Song Wreaking Havoc at Happywoods* on her bed, using the two sheets as curtains. This was my first attempt at artistic activities. However, right now I was offstage in the narrow aisle barely one meter in width. If I turned around, my bags would bang into the boards on both sides, and the Bright formula milk bottles, dating back to the 1950s, that I was using to store the chili sauce and fried pork might crack.

Bright formula milk was said to be my major source of nutrition between weaning and three years of age. The thick glass bottles had waffle squares around the neck and on the bottom. Form was surely quality assurance for content. Growing up on such a high-quality diet, I was always confident in my intelligence. Although I had consumed many bottles of formula, there were only three or four bottles left now. The rest had been ruined by my rolling them on the floor like toy cars. Back then, Grandpa, with his monthly salary over eighty yuan, had provided well for our family of five. The period shortly after the Liberation was the golden age for me as well as for him. The pity was I didn't have any recollection. Ever since I was able to remember things, our family had been coming down in the world at an accelerating speed until I, the one expected to be the next bread earner, had to leave home to till farm somewhere else. There was no knowing whether the downward trajectory had come to an end. A line of poetry came to mind: "Crossing the Sanggan River a second time, I look back at Bingzhou. Having lived there for ten years, I regret to part with my second hometown." Compared to the bleak prospects ahead, the deteriorating life I had led so far might be a golden age once more. I had to turn around and have a final good look. Who cared if the glass bottles broke?

I turned around. The bottles were all right, a good omen.

The florescent lamp was on. Its achromatic light pulsed at a high frequency. The eyes of my grandparents seemed to be watery. I didn't think they cried. It must be the lighting, my emotions and myopia. The numerous auspicious remarks they had uttered were still ringing in my ears. Grandma had gotten up at 4 a.m., started the kitchen fire and cooked six poached eggs for me. Six was the lucky number in our family, because its pronunciation was similar to "smoothness." My seat number in middle school had been 26, which was on one hand disheartening because it has two prime factors—2 and 13, but comforting on the other hand, because at least there was a 6. Probably I was a blockhead with some good fortune, which was at least better than being an unfortunate smart guy.

On my birthday every year since I was ten, they had always made me eat six eggs. Think about it in another way. The six eggs on my birthday in 1960 cost them three yuan (market price, not ration price), one tenth of Grandpa's monthly pension and three times the average daily food expenditure of our entire household. Now you can fully appreciate the lengths my grandparents went to solicit good luck. But then, this became a reason I doubted their devotion to the Goddess of Mercy. If everyone could say or do things for good luck, why bother worshiping the Goddess and doing good? If we had to say or do things to avoid bad luck, then the Goddess didn't seem omnipotent. Growing up with my grandparents, I had long been exposed to such religious concepts as karma, predestination, offering sacrifices to receive blessings and evade calamity, a good deed as credit to the doer in the next life, and auspicious remarks. I had dismissed them because they were full of loopholes and self-contradictions.

Years later, when I mentioned this to a devout Christian several years my junior, he attributed it to my not having cultivated myself sufficiently in my previous life. Since I was heavy, I might have been a butcher in my previous life. A person well cultivated in his previous life was transported by religion. Religion spoke to the heart, not to the mind. The mind could grasp the world, but not God who created the world. I started to have a taste of religious transport. Still later, I repeated these remarks to Hong Liu, who had studied religion on his own and was ready to apply to a graduate level program in religion. He dismissed my Christian friend as a sham, because self-cultivation and past lives were both Buddhist concepts. There are Heaven and Hell in Christianity, but not reincarnation. What matters to Christians is the Last Judgment, a one-off event that prescribes either annihilation or immortality, period. While the religions of the world generally reject reason, some sects under their umbrella invariably flaunt rationality. My sense of religious transport was heightened.

My grandparents had apparently cultivated themselves well in the previous life. In their eyes, there was nothing contradictory in believing in karma, fate, self-cultivation, and the solicitation of good luck. In fact, they thought the two complemented each other like meat and vegetables. In their determination to make that morning as auspicious as possible, they didn't allow themselves to cry. They were laughing. Grandpa's toothless laughter sounded like bells from a temple shrouded in fog. He was happy. He had gotten up at a quarter past four, groped around, and then came to wake me up. I was wide awake. In fact I doubted if I had slept at all, but, not wishing to add to the load on his mind, I pretended to be woken. As soon as I got dressed, Grandpa dragged me to the black enamel glass case on top of which the statue of the Goddess of Mercy stood. A fake rosewood end table had been laid out in front for the occasion. On it was an incense burner converted from a rusty cigarette tin and a box of incense sticks. Three incense sticks had been unwrapped. On the lid of the box was printed "Indian Agalloch Eaglewood Incense." It must be Grandpa's stock for critical events. Although he had said that "People's Sanitary Incense" was just another name, more appropriate for the time being, for "Indian Agalloch Eaglewood Incense," this box showed his reservation.

When Grandpa gestured me toward the incense sticks, I

was surprised and hesitant. Multiple emotions darted across his thin face. Well, for the sake of his quivering facial muscles, I'd better compromise. It was just going to be a token of gratitude to my grandparents. Starting from 1965, in front of our neighbors, my grandparents defended their sacrificial meals to the ancestors with a "modernized" script: This is just an expression of regard by the living to the deceased. So I would express my regard now. I kindled the three incense sticks, snuffed out the fire like Grandpa used to do, made three bows with my hands folded in front, prayed, planted the incense sticks in the burner, and bowed three more times. Grandpa was satisfied with the way I conducted myself. He would have been even more satisfied if he knew that I had prayed for his, and Grandma's, longevity.

There was a tale in *A Collection of Daredevil Stories* that went as follows: A man lay a wooden statue of a deity across a ditch as a footbridge. Another man cried out that this was a sin. He restored the statue to its pedestal in a dilapidated temple. A third man, known as Ai Zi, passed by the temple and overheard the deity tell his attending ghost that he was going to punish the man who had carried him back. The ghost asked why. The deity said, "Punishment won't work on the first guy because he has no faith. My fury can only be felt by my believers." It was too late for me to declare my faith in the Goddess of Mercy now, so I had prayed for her blessing on her longtime followers—my grandparents.

I looked back with difficulty, managing to see nothing but my grandparents' seemingly watery eyes. My eyes lingered on them for a mere second, because I didn't want them to misinterpret it as my unwillingness to part. Then they might break down and ruin the auspicious atmosphere. Looking ahead, I moved toward the door my mother held open for me. My grandparents saw me off at the landing. Not wishing to disturb our neighbors, they bade me goodbye with eyes and gestures. Grandpa broke the silence as I was about to turn a corner. "Write to us as soon as you arrive!"

Grandma added immediately, "Don't save your pennies. Health first!"

Mother and I stepped into the street. It was pitch dark. I was reminded of the name of a play—*Break the Darkness before Dawn*. Mother's Swiss-made woman's wristwatch pointed at 4:45. This watch, five years my senior, was the only portable timepiece in our family. The cool night air was refreshing. Having always been a nocturnal animal, I dreaded getting up at 5 a.m. and lights out at 8 p.m. on the farm. The cool refreshing air gave me the confidence that I would cope with it after a while. From now on, I was going to lead an independent life out there. I must turn over a new leaf. The conditions couldn't be better. In a place where nobody knew me, I could have a fresh start. Rogues and thugs were inconsequential. I must grit my teeth and charge ahead. A new and better life was beckoning.

I fell silent. My mother walked behind me. We didn't talk much. It suddenly occurred to me that we had always been like this. And it also had always been the case between me and my grandparents. I didn't feel like telling them things unless it was highly necessary, like Mr. Jin's hospitalization or my decision to go to Hong Liu's farm, or unless they pressed. I was a man of few words. What a disturbing thought! No, I wasn't always reticent, because at least I talked to my siblings. Somehow I had associated taciturnity with aloofness, which was quiet undesirable in the current context. But since when did I become silent in the company of adults? Probably it started with my younger sister's going to primary school when I was a fifth grader. She was such a bore at that time, chattering about trifles at school, first with Grandma and then Mother. Consequently they knew more about her classmates than would a personnel cadre. Or had I turned weird even earlier? Had I been born unsociable? This was not right. I must talk to Mother. But to talk about what? It was not easy to strike up a conversation. Funny, why didn't Mother talk either? I looked back at her. Her slightly yellow pupils glittered with earnestness and confidence, like two lamps in the vast shadow of night. I felt at ease. She didn't talk because she was confident that I would never associate with thugs on the farm, and she wouldn't give me advice on how to improve my prospects because she didn't think she was any wiser. Her practicality was touching. It worked better on me than a thousand exhortations. I looked back again. She reacted by hurrying up, but then she checked her watch.

"It's still early. Take your time."

I answered, "Okay. I wasn't rushing you. I was checking if you could keep up the pace."

"I'm fine. Shall I carry some luggage for you?"

"No," I said, "I can handle it." Words failed me once more.

We reached Dada Terminal at a quarter past five. The street lamps were still on. The sallow light, the wet cement floor, and the hubbub of voices reminded me of a wet market. I had been to a wet market, where one could buy meat and produce, only once, when I was in fourth grade, saving a place for Grandma in a queue in front of the butcher's counter. This experience had made such a deep impression on me that I deemed it the utmost failure in life for an adult man to shop at the wet market. Badly off as Grandpa was, he never set foot in it. My endeavors in later life were partly driven by the wish to stay away from it. What a symbol it was, taking my first step into the world from a place recalling a wet market!

There were no loud cheers, decorations, banners or slogans at Dada Terminal. Since working in Chongming was nothing compared to permanent residency in remote Heilongjiang or Yunnan province, the authorities hadn't bothered to arrange a send-off for us. In my mind, a boisterous ceremony accompanied by gongs and drums was as unnecessary as the tearless howl of a bride before entering her sedan chair in the traditonal wedding ceremonies. Nevertheless the absence of such formalities today made me feel despondent. Zhuge Liang should be blamed for corrupting the minds of the Chinese literati. Before him, learned men had been down to earth and called a spade a spade. After him, they put on airs to lure rulers to come begging and offer them high positions in the government. The exemplary power of Zhuge Liang was so great that over a thousand years, hypocrisy became second nature to Chinese intellectuals. Just look at me. Serving for two years as class representative to our Chinese teacher had been enough to teach me not to say what I thought.

The waiting lounge had not filled up yet. I settled down in some vacant seats at the end of the first row of chairs. Mother refused to leave me there. Instead she sat across from me. I didn't know what else to say. The more I tried, the more tongue-tied I became. Conversations in Chongming dialect grew louder and louder, like waves lapping at rocks. All my knowledge of the dialect had come from Shanghai farce. Chongming natives were said to end each spoken sentence with a modal particle that sounded like "crab" in Shanghai dialect. Therefore they had the nickname, "Chongming Crabs." Having never met a Chongming native in my eighteen years of life, I was overwhelmed by the number of them in the lounge and the booming voices they seemed all to possess. My eavesdropping taught me the following things: Firstly, when a Chongming native met another Chongming native outside Chongming (including in Shanghai), they hit if off immediately. The dialect seemed to be their bonding agent. Secondly, Chongming natives maintained their rich accent even if they had been traveling extensively, joined the army, worked in strategic areas in the Chinese hinterland, or studied and worked in northern China. In all my four subsequent years in Chongming, I never met a local who spoke standard Mandarin. In conclusion, Chongming dialect was harder to break than not only Shanghai dialect but also those of Ningbo and Suzhou city of Jiangsu province. By inference, speakers of such a dialect were more cohesive as a group and hostile toward outsiders.

Anxiety crept into my mind. I had ignored a threat, a psychological barrier created by regional and linguistic differences. Perhaps it was more essential for me to win support from the natives than to get along well with thugs. The poor and lower-middle class peasants on the farm represented the establishment. If I got cornered by thugs, they would be my only saviors. If I wanted to make a difference in the future, they would be my only backers. The problem was they were Chongming natives, whose dialect jarred my nerves upon first contact, like a coquettish woman. I guess this went both ways. To the Chongming natives, their dialect must be the most pleasant and unpretentious in the country, and Shanghai dialect, the source of much annoyance. Plus, the reputation of Shanghai natives in other parts of China had gone from bad to worse in recent years. A scholar knew all the wide world's affairs without having to step outside his gate. I was aware how fellow countrymen thought of us Shanghai natives as cunning and how they avoided us like plague.

Although Chongming was administratively part of Shanghai, its residents, unlike natives of other suburban counties, always stressed their distinctive identity. The psychological barrier between Chongming natives and Shanghai natives might be no less daunting than that between Europeans and Asians. Would I be able to overcome it? Would I be able to eliminate my inborn aversion to them and would they do the same with me? These thoughts made me sick at heart, as if I had eaten too much heavy food. I must fight my way through. I composed myself. The first step would be to join their conversation, but Mother's presence was inconvenient so I demanded firmly that she leave. She complied this time.

As soon as she left, I turned my attention to a neighboring young Chongming native in a bluish gray uniform. My first question to him was whether the ship to Chongming jolted a lot, a question of top concern to me since I was prone to motion sickness. The outlook was worsened by the fact that I had hardly slept during the night. I would hate to throw up in front of Jing and other strangers. The young man from Chongming responded warmly. Later I found out that Chongming natives were always courteous to others. Their courtesy masked a strong sense of inferiority, which give the impression of being sly. The

Chongming natives I would come to know were neither like crabs running wild nor cunning foxes. They were more like rabbits—docile, alert, but a bit timid. I wondered why history had shown that quite a number of Chongming natives had become pirates, because they appeared to me to be law-abiding citizens. Suzhou natives were known for being mild, but I thought Chongming natives outperformed them.

I struck up a conversation with the young Chongming native in the waiting lounge, with a view of establishing rapport with some peasants as soon as possible. Gradually I picked up a bit of the Chongming accent. I didn't do this to tease but to conform. I was a natural. The realization put me on top of the world. This was indeed a running start. My intuition at the waiting lounge turned out to be right over the next four years, because, despite setbacks and spectacles, I was able to attain my goals relatively quickly and go back to Shanghai for good. As I was beaming and talking, my new friend's eyes strayed over my head. I thought he had spotted an acquaintance, but no, it was my mother.

"Look out. Catch!"

I had hardly turned around when I saw, out of the corner of my eye, a greasy steel-gray package hurtling at me. My palms were burned so badly that I almost dropped it. Mother's panic-stricken voice exacerbated the tension, "Don't pinch them! There's soup inside!"

A package of steamed buns, fried and fresh out of the pan.

I tossed the package between my two hands like a ball. Mother said, "They are from a famous food stall nearby. I saw a long queue in front of it. They put meat jelly in it to make a delicious soup when it's steamed. I don't think six eggs were enough for a breakfast. Oh my, the queue moved so slowly. I worried that I was going to miss you. I ran all the way back. Oh, my hands! But never mind. Eat them while they're hot. Don't let the soup become jelly again."

Never before had I felt my mother's love so deeply. Not knowing how to express my gratitude, I suppressed it.

It transformed into hatred. I hated her for making me into a sheltered plant in the hothouse in front of my peasant comrades. Having no vent for the hatred, I turned to attack the steamed buns. Remorse arose when the number of buns had gone down to two: I was more than full while Mother had not had a bite. She was going home to the usual breakfast—soupy rice. But with only two buns left, it was too late to remember manners.

Apparently deeming she had earned it, Mother sat down again.

People became restless at ten to six. They gathered up their luggage and moved past me to the gate. I stood up to look for Jing. At six o'clock sharp, boarding started. A steward came to rope off the first row of seats. We were to board ahead of other rows. Seated passengers rose to their feet and pressed ahead. Jing was nowhere to be seen. I stepped onto a seat to have a better view. The steward scolded me in a loud voice. But I had caught sight of Jing in the front of the third row, so I called out in an even louder voice. Seeing me, Jing threaded his way toward us, but the angry steward refused to let him come ahead. The cigarette Jing offered was ignored. I had to introduce Jing to my mother over the rows. They exchanged pleasantries. Then he shook hands with Mother and me. We agreed to meet onboard. He went back to his row. Mother and I hurried out. We were the only few left in the first row. Once out in the open air, the foul smell of the Huangpu River reached my nostrils. My stomach, which was bulging with steamed buns, started to churn. Shanghai wanted to use her ugly side to scare me away forever, like Dame Camille did with Armand. But I had seen through her, and this was my parting vow to her: I'll be back. Wait for me. The sea may run dry and the rocks may crumble, but I'll love you until the end of time. The Huangpu River may stink of rotten fish, but I'll be back. As proof of my unchanging fidelity, I took a huge gulp of the stinky air.

The railing that guarded the pontoon came into sight. Mother spoke all of a sudden, "I don't like Jing very much."

"Why?"

"Hard to say. He seems to have a high opinion of himself." Surprised by her acumen, which she must have gotten from Grandpa, I regretted introducing Jing to her. Mother spoke again, "Take care." I said, "I will. But a first impression may be wrong." Mother nodded. "Take care, anyway."

We approached the railing. Only passengers were allowed to go through. I waved goodbye.

The crowd tore me from her onto the ship.

In another couple of moments, I was nudged into the bottom compartment, a place that was to be transformed into a dark hideous cave in my subconscious, often looming toward the end of my nightmares.

As is known to experienced travelers, the bottom compartment is the worst seating area possible. Since it was a short haul to Chongming and the ship was quite small, tickets were all priced the same. Passengers had raced each other in order to board first and get the best seats, except for me. I congratulated myself on being the only passenger in the bottom compartment, where I could choose my seat at leisure. At the same time I took pity on those fellow passengers. whose feet were trampling the sheet-iron ceiling above my head like war drums. What was the fuss about? Why didn't they come down? Was I wrong? No, they were wrong. First of all, according to geometric principles, the ship rocked less in the lower parts. Secondly, according to the principles of physics, the bottom compartment was definitely warmer than the cabins on the upper deck. "Knowledge is power." How true the saying is!

I hoped Jing would come soon. Otherwise it would be hard for me to defend multiple seats against the rest of the throng. I leaned against a wall listening to the non-stop drum beat above. It was some time before a pair of feet clambered down the iron stairs, and then came a trickle of others. But all in all, passengers were not eager to come down and nobody challenged me. I fidgeted. Although Truth was often in the hands of the minority, the minority did hope to gather followers. Solitude was always the most intolerable to an ambitious person, while at the same time it was his greatest attraction. I waited for ages. Jing didn't show up. I asked my neighbors the time, but none of them had a watch, which was quite common at that time, because a Shanghai Brand watch was a good betrothal gift from a bridegroom to the bride's family. Actually, even if I had the time, waiting was still the only option. Without time as a reference, I suddenly felt an immense, unexplainable threat to my own existence. I lost patience with sitting. The portholes attracted my attention. I went over and peered out. Turbid river water splashed against the dark blue glass pane, leaving behind earthworm-like stains. We were submerged in the water, an alarming realization as I remembered Grandma's remark that people who slept on the stomach ended up drowning.

Jing materialized when I was nearly consumed with despair. From afar he shouted, "Why are you here? I've been looking for you up there!" I explained why the bottom compartment was better from the perspectives of geometry and physics. He smiled, seemingly impressed. Then he said, "They're all up there, Zheng Guomei and the others. Care to join us?" I asked if there was room up there. He said no but we could manage by sitting on a bag. I said, "It's better for you to come down. Roomier here." "Okay," he said, "right after the ship sails." He turned to ascend the stairs because many fellow students had come to see them off. I declined his invitation to go up with him. Instead I urged him to move his luggage down right away. Otherwise I was afraid the seats would be taken.

Sure enough, Jing moved his luggage down at once. He also brought another person with him, a guy he called Moustache, although the said object was just a tuft of darkish hair right below his nostrils. He introduced Moustache as the best friend and classmate of Wang Ling, a Red Guards Platoon Leader in their faction. Wang Ling was sitting with Zheng Guomei. Both expected to meet me on the upper deck. Since Moustache had failed to find a seat up there, he was going to sit here in the bottom compartment. Moustache offered a hand to me. Handshaking seemed to be the fad, a fact I must bear in mind. Jing asked me again if I'd like to tour the upper deck. I again said no. He left with Moustache.

Jing lingered a long time on the upper deck. I sat like Rodin's *The Thinker* surrounded by bags, but I was not thinking at all. The world around me was as sleepy as the lights in the cabin. Sitting was good. There was no need to think and nothing to think about. I fell asleep with my eyes open.

Jing showed up again. He chattered cheerfully at me, "Why didn't you go up? Your mother was standing there the whole time."

"What?" I asked. "Is she still there?"

"No. We've already passed the Waibaidu Bridge."

"What? The ship has sailed?"

"Sure. Didn't you know? Didn't you hear the whistle? Didn't you feel the jolt?"

"No. Nothing at all."

"Listen. Aren't the engines loud?"

"Is that the engines? It was there when I came in. Where did she stand? Where did my mother stand? I thought only passengers were allowed on the pontoon."

"They all stood near the cement parapet."

"Did she see you?"

"Yes."

"Did she say anything?"

"Sound couldn't carry that far. She waved at me. I waved back."

I resented Jing. Had my mother stood in the bitter cold only to be able to wave at him? I hadn't gone up because I didn't know she had lingered. Why didn't he tell me? He didn't even need to climb down. Just shout from the hatch opening. A matter of only one minute!

"Why didn't you go up?" Jing was still grinning.

"How could I leave? What about these bags?"

"What's the big deal? There's nothing valuable. And a thief has no way to get out. Chongming is our last and only destination."

Jing offered to take me up to meet Zheng Guomei and Wang Ling. I refused to leave the bags unattended. Surrendering to my obstinacy, he promised to find Moustache to relieve me.

Mother had stood by the parapet straining her eyes at our ship, but I was nowhere to be seen. Whistles shrieked. Our ship pulled out. People around her waved frantically at it, tears streaming down their cheeks, as if they were Red Guards receiving an audience with Chairman Mao. She stood there not uttering a word, her reversible jacket as dark as the night, her hands folded on her lower abdomen, and her fingers greasy from handling the buns. Her eyes were two dry wells, her eyelashes quivering like wild grass around them.

There was a pinch at the root of my nose. Intuitively I opened my mouth wide, licking my lower lip. It worked. The pinch went away. There must be a mysterious passageway between the salivary glands and tear glands, I said to myself.

Moustache poked his head through the hatch opening. "Hey. Come up. I'll be there in a sec." We passed each other on the stairs. It didn't occur to me to ask until I had reached the opening, "Where are they?"

"Just look ahead. They're there." I had no idea which direction to look, but I was too embarrassed to ask again.

I approached the side of the ship. A gust of wind blew in my face. We were passing cement matchbox-like houses onshore. On my field trips to gain industrial production experience as part of the secondary school curriculum, I had learned they were all warehouses for the Shanghai Port. I wondered which zone they were in. Anyway there was no scenery to gawk at in this area. I went to the other side of the ship, which faced Pudong, the less developed part of Shanghai on the other side of the Huangpu. Instead of tall buildings there was only a long stretch of brown land. What a shock to lose sight of bustling Shanghai in such a short time! I searched the cabin on the ship's bow. They were not there. I went to the cabin sternward. There they were.

Jing pointed out a tall woman, "This is Zheng Guomei."

Was she the woman Hong Liu was in love with? I tried hard not to show surprise. At first sight she looked like a middle-aged woman, not a young lady. There were two explanations. For one thing, she was tall. She was probably 168 centimeters in height, while Hong Liu's height, even after some inflation, was a mere 170 centimeters. For another, she was plump. No, she was not obese. Her figure was still well proportioned. It was just that her sausage-like arms, waist and thighs were on the verge of bursting her clothes open. I could almost hear the fabric groan. The two short plaits didn't add to her charm. Instead they looked like some desperate attempt to keep a youthful look. Rude as it was, I checked out her face, hoping to find out why Hong Liu fancied her. Hong Liu had once said she had a perfectly oval face, the shape of a goose egg. I couldn't tell if it was true since I had never seen a goose egg. Maybe goose eggs were flatter and rounder than chicken eggs or duck eggs. However I did spot a resemblance to a hot water bottle. No wonder "Hot Water Bottle" was one of her nicknames. She had regular but ordinary features. A mole stood out below her left eyelid. Later I understood that Hong Liu thought highly of the mole. It was known as a beauty spot. In Balzac's *Cousin Bette*, the coquettish Valerie stuck a black silk patch on her face to pass as a beauty spot. However back then I was too dense to appreciate it. Instead I considered it the last straw. Anyway, I admired Hong Liu even more, because young as he was, he had learned not to judge people by their appearance. Throughout the ages, many men had failed to attain such a lofty realm of thought. As the expression goes, "It's natural that a hero loves beauty."

Jing went on to introduce me to Wang Ling. He was the only person not to offer a handshake. If he was one size bigger, his sullen face and the fluffy fleece collar on his yellow military uniform would have made him the perfect bully. Only later did I find out that he was actually a quiet, honest guy. Because he was quiet and honest, he had to wear protection.

Probably piqued by my sizing her up, Zheng Guomei didn't wait long to ask me, "Why did you decide to go with Lacey?" I couldn't come up with a reply. She laughed heartily. "Are you sad that Lacey is not coming?" She didn't beat about the bush. Could I act the same with her? No. She was even more amused, narrowing her eyes. "Don't worry. Lacey has entrusted you to us. Our company is as good as his."

The verb "entrust" was too much for me to swallow. Jing stood by grinning, as if he deferred to Zheng Guomei. After a while I said goodbye to them. When I reached the bottom compartment, the verb "entrust" was stuck inside my chest.

Moustache had deserted his post.

An inexplicable anger flared up in me, but I managed to put it out. I couldn't afford to lose my temper with anyone. Someone started to sing, "Great is the sky, great is the earth, but the Party's love for us is even greater. Dear is my mother, dear is my father, but Chairman Mao is dearer to all of us . . ."

I took the *Three Hundred Tang Poems* out of my bag. I must not fritter away my time. I must seize every opportunity to study. However I couldn't take in the words. Then I decided to use the book to divine the future. I closed the book, laid my right hand on it, and prayed, "God, Jesus, Sakyamuni, Jade Emperor, Allah, Goddess of Mercy, Lord Lao Zi, Zeus, Jupiter, and whichever deity is listening, please give your humble servant a sign in this book so that he knows where his future lies."

After the prayer, I flipped the book open at random and read the first poem on the right-hand page. It was page 72. The first four lines of Du Fu's *A Song of an Old Cypress*: "Beside the temple of the Great Premier stands an ancient cypress, with a trunk of green bronze and a root of stone. The girth of its wide bark would be the reach of forty men, and its tip of kingfisher blue is two thousand feet in heaven."

"The Great Premier," "an ancient cypress," "a root of stone" and "two thousand feet" all seemed to be good omens. I decided to try again and use the first poem on the left-hand page as reference. Page 205, *A Sigh in the Spring Palace* by Du Xunhe: "Knowing beauty my misfortune, I face my mirror with a sigh. To please a fastidious emperor, how shall I array myself?"

Neither the title nor the opening was auspicious. To which beauty was it referring? Could Dong Yiren possibly be a beauty? The annotation read: "The poet compared himself to a courtesan. He composed this poem to express his resentment." This fit my current situation but I didn't wish to harbor a lifelong resentment. I would have another go and stick to the right-hand page. If there were two poems on the same page, the second one would count. Page 180. Indeed there were two poems, the bottom one being Du Fu's *On Leaving the Tomb of Premier Fang*: "Having to travel back now to this far place, I dismount beside your lonely tomb ..." Well, they were getting worse. Not taking my defeat lying down, I flipped again and again. I had never browsed this book so intensively. The results boded ill rather than well. Then it dawned on me that this was the wrong book for divination. Good Tang dynasty poets wrote about people's suffering, bad ones voiced their sorrow at parting. Both were in low spirits, unaware that with passion and struggle, they could realize a brilliant future. Since they were hardly optimistic, how could I derive a bright outlook for myself from their poems? I'd fare better with a copy of *The Red Sun Shining over Anyuan.* What a pity I didn't have it with me!

My bladder was bursting. Neither Jing nor Moustache was likely to come to my rescue. I steeled myself to ask a neighbor to keep an eye on our bags. Once out of the restroom, I decided to have a look at the sea. After all, this was my first voyage and a milestone in my life. I needed something to tell my grandson when I was old. Have a look. Forget about the bottles and scruffy clothes for a while. I craned my neck left and right. To the west, fields stretched as far as the eye could see, dotted with houses here and there. To the east, the brown stretch of land had been replaced by a vast expanse of water. I was sure we were out on the sea. The water was still yellow but different from river water. I stooped over the railing. The snowy breakers sloshing around the ship looked like lard on a split pork belly. The water was much darker, stickier and denser, like syrup. It must be the greater specific gravity of sea water.

Moustache came over with a cigarette dangling from his lips. He dug out a packet of Flying Horse Brand cigarettes from his pocket and offered one to me as a kind of apology. I declined. He asked brazenly who was with the bags. I said, "No one. I had to use the toilet." He said, "Never mind. Let them be." I said, "The sea water looks dense. Its specific gravity must be greater." He said, "What are you talking about? We are not out of Wusongkou yet." To tell the truth, I had never heard of Wusongkou. But I was smart enough to deduce that it must be the river mouth. He had a smile on his face. If only I could bite my tongue off.

I went back to the bottom compartment, sank among the bags, and cursed myself.

Noises started to penetrate the bubble I had created around myself. Several youths on their way to the farm were asking questions of a middle-aged woman. The tip of her bobbed hair had wilted. Her face was the color of her threadbare Lenin coat. She cupped her jaw with a hand as if nursing a toothache. Her low voice floated over the nonstop roar of engines like a white sail on the sea, and her eyes were two eagles gliding around the sail without seemingly doing so. She emitted a kind of faint aura that made me aware of the weight of the turbid, dark gray air on me and drew my attention to her.

Someone asked her which was better in a dormitory, the upper berth or the lower berth of a bunk bed. She said each had its pros and cons. With an upper berth, it was inconvenient to climb up and down, but it was cleaner and more private if you let down your mosquito net. On the other hand, it was convenient sleeping in the lower berth, but your sheets got soiled more quickly because others tended to sit on it. It was a bad idea to keep down the mosquito net all the time. Since there were no stools in the dormitory, you distanced yourself from others if you didn't allow them to sit on your bed. Some people at her school for cadres laid out a towel on top of their bed to sit on, but still it was not enough.

She shared her insights in an unhurried way. The more I listened, the more afraid I became. The more afraid I was, the more I wanted to hear. It was just like listening to ghost stories. Seriously, if so much thinking had to go into the choice of a bed, how many more grim issues awaited me on that vast alien land!

I had a headache. My thick, dark hair seemed to want to tear away from my miserable head. Without my knowing, my right hand had ploughed it several times. I raised it before my eyes. Twining between my fingers were withered black bodies sprinkled with snowflakes.

Someone clambered down the stairs shouting, "We're out of Wusongkou!" The people who had sought advice from the middle-aged woman all ran up to the deck. The guy to whom I had entrusted our bags a while before asked me to keep an eye on his bags. I obliged. The middle-aged cadre was left alone. She lay down on an unoccupied bench, trying to have a nap with a bag as her pillow. Although I had a lot of questions, I thought it better not to disturb her.

After a long while, my fellow passengers had enough of the ocean view and returned. I went up. So this was the real thing! The sea water was a white stretch, joining the sky at the horizon. Our ship was the only moving object except for those endless waves. Without the white foam under the ship, I could have hardly told whether the ship was moving or not.

A heroic sense seized me.

Open sea, here I come! World, here I am!

Only later did I learn that what I had seen was not the sea but the Yangtze River. Chongming is an island with the sea on one side, but you can't actually view the sea when coming from Shanghai.

Stories by Contemporary Writers from Shanghai

A Pair of Jade Frogs
Ye Xin

Ah, Blue Bird
Lu Xing'er

Beautiful Days
Teng Xiaolan

Between Confidantes
Chen Danyan

Calling Back the Spirit of the Dead
Peng Ruigao

Dissipation
Tang Ying

Folk Song
Li Xiao

Forty Roses
Sun Yong

Game Point
Xiao Bai

Gone with the River Mist
Yao Emei

Goodby, Xu Hu!
Zhao Changtian

His One and Only
Wang Xiaoyu

Labyrinth of the Past
Zhang Yiwei

Memory and Oblivion
Wang Zhousheng

No Sail on the Western Sea
Ma Yuan

Normal People
Shen Shanzeng

Paradise on Earth
Zhu Lin

Platinum Passport
Zhu Xiaolin

River under the Eaves
Yin Huifen

She She
Zou Zou

The Confession of a Bear
Sun Wei

The Elephant
Chen Cun

The Little Restaurant
Wang Anyi

The Messenger's Letter
Sun Ganlu

The Most Beautiful Face in the World
Xue Shu

There Is No If
Su De

Vicissitudes of Life
Wang Xiaoying

When a Baby Is Born
Cheng Naishan

White Michelia
Pan Xiangli